'Seems we've learnt quite a bit about each other in the past twenty-four hours, haven't we?'

'Yes. I suppose so.'

'And one of the things I've learnt about you, Kerry, is that you're one feisty woman.'

His arm was still around her, holding her against him, and he leant forward and brushed her forehead with his lips. She didn't draw back. Rather, she allowed herself to imagine the sweetness of his mouth on hers—because wasn't this secretly what she had been longing for, perhaps even needing?

In the back of her mind a little voice whispered, *You're mad—you've only known this guy for two days!* Whatever Denovan said, they were still almost strangers. She didn't know his background, or what sadness he referred to in his past, and he'd only brushed his lips across her forehead, but in that moment she realised that she had been attracted to him from the first moment she'd seen him.

She pressed her lips to his cheek, responding to his feather-light kiss with eagerness, giving in to the clamour of her own longing. A kind of dizzy freedom from the sadness and constraints of the past year swept through her, and she couldn't help her response—an almost compulsive need to make love to this man she'd only known for such a short time.

Dear Reader

The idea for this story came from reading about a family feud and how it affected the other people involved. I wondered how it might impinge on the lives of two people in love if they were caught up in a feud—could it ruin their future? Or would they be able to overcome all obstacles and find future happiness together?

I set the story in the beautiful countryside of the Peak District, although Braxton Falls is an imaginary village. I hope I've brought a flavour of the area to the story, and the sense of community that binds a small place together in adversity.

I so enjoyed writing this story—I hope you will find pleasure in reading it.

Best wishes

Judy

CELEBRITY IN BRAXTON FALLS

BY
JUDY CAMPBELL

Judy Campbell is from Cheshire. As a teenager she spent a great year at high school in Oregon, USA, as an exchange student. She has worked in a variety of jobs, including teaching young children, being a secretary and running a small family business. Her husband comes from a medical family, and one of their three grown-up children is a GP. Any spare time—when she's not writing romantic fiction—is spent playing golf, especially in the Highlands of Scotland.

CHAPTER ONE

'GOLDEN sands fringed by waving palms, an azure sea and balmy days that you will love...'

The photograph of an idyllic beach scene underneath the caption in the brochure looked impossibly alluring—Kerry Latimer could almost feel the texture of the warm sand between her toes, imagine the limpid water lapping against her body, the sun sparkling on the waves, palm trees rustling in the light wind...

'Too right I'd love it,' she muttered wryly, then tore the brochure firmly in two, crushing it into a ball and flinging it sadly into the waste-paper basket. 'A shame I won't be going to the golden sands and azure sea after all...'

She looked bleakly through the surgery window, made blurry by the lashing rain, and at the dark sky outside, with the glowering shadows on the hills in the distance. During the past few days there had been a continuous torrential downpour, and the river flowing through the village was ominously high—a world away from dreamy islands in the middle of the Caribbean and their sunny climes. If only Frank had been more careful. If only he'd slowed down a bit, she would be almost there by now.

The horribly expensive pale coral silk dress hanging in its clear plastic cover on the wall of the surgery caught her eye—at this very moment she ought to have been on a plane, tossing back champagne as she winged her way to her cousin's wedding in Tobago, looking forward to wearing the dress later that week as one of her cousin's bridesmaids. Now, of course, after what had happened, she was stuck at work in Braxton Falls for the foreseeable future, covering for Frank, any hope of jetting off to beautiful sun-kissed beaches absolutely scuppered.

'Just my luck that my first holiday after a year's hard grind should be hijacked.' Kerry sighed—there was nothing she could do about the situation but grit her teeth and bear it, as her mother used to say.

She picked up the phone on her desk, and stabbed out a number. 'Hello?' she said as it was answered. 'Is that Denovan O'Mara? This is Kerry Latimer. I'm a colleague of your brother's at The Larches Medical Centre. I'm afraid that I've some bad news about him…' She took a deep breath and said gently, 'I'm very sorry to tell you that Frank was in a car accident last night and was seriously injured.'

There was a second's silence—Kerry imagined the shock Denovan would feel as he received the information about his half-brother, and she waited for the appalled intake of breath at the news, the concerned enquiry about his condition.

The reply sounded exasperated rather than anxious. 'The stupid fool—what the hell was he doing?'

Kerry stared at the phone, rather taken aback—it seemed a callous response to such awful news. 'We think Frank touched the accelerator instead of the brake—it's an automatic car—and he went through the garage door and out of the back wall of the garage down a steep incline, hitting a tree.'

A derisive short laugh. 'I don't suppose I'm all that surprised—it's typical of him. I always knew Frank was an accident waiting to happen—he's impatient and reckless. Were any other people injured?'

'No,' she answered coldly. 'No one else was involved.'

'Well, that's a blessing—he's an awful driver.' Privately Kerry agreed with Denovan—Frank always seemed to be taking corners too fast and scraping his car, or denting his bumpers when he reversed.

'So where is he now?' asked Denovan briskly.

'He's in the local hospital at the moment, but will probably be transferred to Derby for further detailed trauma scans. He has serious injuries to his head and a very bruised back. He's stable but in an induced coma. I thought I should let you know as I believe you're his only relative.'

'I see. Well, I suppose I'll have to come up then, although it's highly inconvenient. I could really do without this.'

'Excuse me?' What was this man like, and how self-centred could you be, weighing inconvenience with seeing a desperately ill brother? Kerry felt a slow burn of anger. If anyone should feel aggrieved, it was she, Kerry Latimer—obliged to cancel her holiday at the last minute, and then having to hold the fort at a two-handed medical practice for the foreseeable future.

Denovan's voice sounded tetchy. 'I'm in negotiations for a new contract and it could be rather tricky to leave at the moment.' Then he added unenthusiastically, 'But I will come up, of course.'

'If you think you can spare the time,' said Kerry sarcastically. 'He is very poorly, you know.'

'I'm sure he is. Sounds as if he'll be out of commission for a while—that won't make your job any easier, I guess,' he conceded. 'I'll be up when I've finished the programme this morning. I should be in Braxton later this afternoon.'

'I'm sure he'll be delighted to see you when he comes round.'

There was a short mirthless laugh at the other end of the line. 'You think?'

'Of course he will!' said Kerry rather indignantly. 'I assume you'll stay at his house?'

'I'll stay in the local hotel—what's it called? The Pear Tree?'

'Do you want me to book you a room?'

The voice softened. 'That's kind of you. One night will do. And it was good of you to let me know about Frank, I appreciate it. I'll see you when I arrive.'

The phone clicked and Kerry leaned back in her chair, frowning, and tapped a pencil against her teeth. She wasn't quite sure what to make of Denovan O'Mara—known to a huge following of adoring fans as 'TV's Dr Medic', helped in no small part by his good looks and knowledgeable, kindly manner.

Kerry grimaced—she felt she'd seen the real Denovan O'Mara a few seconds ago, and it revealed the flipside to his smooth public image—an impatient, irritable and arrogant side. And talk about unsympathetic. If he was as unfeeling as he seemed to be with his brother's plight, what was his bedside manner like with patients?

She'd never actually met Denovan face-to-face, just seen him occasionally on some morning break-fast show, giving his opinion and advice on the latest medical news story or answering viewers' concerns—every inch the glamorous and dreamy TV celebrity doctor with trademark tousled dark hair and piercing blue eyes. His strong, aquiline features regularly ap-peared on magazine covers, his advice was given in many newspaper articles and, in fact, he seemed to be always in the public eye, but from the conversation she'd just had with him, Kerry wasn't sure she was in a hurry to meet him personally.

'Talk about arrogant and selfish,' Kerry muttered as she sorted out the mail left on her desk. 'The guy only seems to think of the inconvenience he's been caused, with not an ounce of sympathy for Frank.'

It was Denovan, the younger of the two brothers, who had the celebrity looks. Frank was a good, reli-able doctor and Kerry had a high opinion of his work, although he had a short fuse, even worse now he was divorced—and perhaps in that respect there was a simi-larity between the two men! Anyway, Kerry could put up with Frank's occasional moods because she loved working in beautiful Braxton Falls.

The brothers certainly didn't appear to be close. As far as she knew, Denovan had never been up to Brax-ton since their father had died six years ago, and Frank rarely spoke of him. Now she came to think of it, the few times she had heard Frank mention his brother, it had been in slightly mocking tones, implying that Denovan thought highly of himself and his celebrity role and was rather a womaniser, never seen with the same girl twice. Having just spoken to Denovan, she thought Frank might have had a point!

Kerry flicked a look at her watch and guiltily started up her computer, clicking on to the patients she had listed for that morning. No good musing about the brothers' relationship with each other—it was nothing to do with her. The list was a full one, reflecting the fact that she'd got some of Frank's patients too—it was going to be a hard slog over the next few weeks, trying to cope by herself without help.

But, boy, was she in need of a holiday. She'd looked forward to being her cousin's bridesmaid for months, and with the wedding set in such an exotic location it had been extra thrilling. It had been something to take her mind off the emotional roller-coaster she'd experienced over the past year. She closed her eyes for a second and swallowed hard, trying to blank out of her mind the heartache and loneliness she'd endured after the shock of Andy's death—at times she wondered if she'd ever get over it. In a world that seemed to be filled with couples it was hard to force herself as a single woman to go out and socialise, and consequently her social life was pretty non-existent. She was getting used to single meals heated up in the microwave. That was why this holiday was going to be such a momentous thing, supposedly kick-starting her to a more positive future. She put all the medical magazines that had arrived to one side and quickly shuffled through the printed emails that had come through with blood-test results and hospital appointments, forcing her mind on to other things. But the incipient headache that had been threatening for some time came on more persistently and she swallowed two painkillers before putting her printouts neatly in her in-tray.

There was a tap on the door, and Daphne Clark, one of the receptionists, came in with a cup of coffee.

'I thought you might need this,' she said. 'After all the excitement last night and getting Frank into hospital you must be exhausted. Have you heard how he is?'

'He may be moved some time today to Derby for further tests, but I can tell you that it'll be a long time before he can get back to work again. I'm on the lookout for a locum urgently, though I doubt I'll get one.' Kerry's voice was gloomy. 'The man that was going to replace me when I was away rang up only yesterday to say he couldn't take the job on after all.'

Daphne shook her head sympathetically as she handed her the coffee. 'It's such a terrible shame about your holiday.'

'If only he'd waited to have this damn accident when I was safely in Tobago!' Kerry said, then she grinned ruefully. 'Oh, no. Forget I said that! Of course I'm very sorry for poor old Frank. He's in a bad way and he certainly didn't mean to crash his car. I guess it was at the end of a long day and he wasn't concentrating.'

'Could you not have gone anyway on a later flight perhaps and asked the medical centre in Laystone to take over?'

'I don't know if they could have taken it on at such short notice, and anyway,' she admitted candidly, 'I couldn't possibly have left Frank, knowing how ill he is.' Kerry took a gulp of the coffee and smiled, raising the cup in salute. 'Now, this is doing me more good than anything could—a large injection of caffeine is just what I needed. And talking of holidays, you might go and put that bridesmaid's dress in its box because every time I see it I want to cry! Oh, and by the way, would you please book a room for Frank's brother at the Pear Tree? He's coming up this afternoon to see Frank.'

Daphne's round face beamed. 'Not the gorgeous Dr Medic? Certainly I will—I shall ask him to give me an autograph for my mother—she's potty about him. Watches every single programme he's on and says he makes her feel better just looking and listening to him.'

Kerry raised an eyebrow. 'He didn't sound all that charming to me. More annoyed that he had to make time to come up here. I think he's a crusty self-centred old bachelor!'

'Don't say that,' protested Daphne, as she walked out. 'I may have been married for seventeen years and have three children, but I can still dream about impossibly handsome men and romance, can't I?'

She unhooked the bridesmaid's dress from the wall and folded it carefully over her arm. 'By the way, Liz Ferris wants you to go and see old Nellie Styles if you can. She had a another fall yesterday and Liz feels she needs an assessment prior to getting some carers in. Of course Nellie won't have it—she told Liz that she wouldn't allow any more community nurses in, she could manage fine by herself and she wasn't having any of those meals on wheels either!'

Kerry laughed. Nellie Styles was a feisty and wilful old lady, but she couldn't help admiring her. 'I'll go at lunchtime,' she promised. 'Then hopefully I'll be back to greet Denovan O'Mara—but I'm not looking forward to it particularly. I have a feeling he and I might not hit it off!'

* * *

Inside Nellie Styles's cottage it was very cold, and there was a general air of neglect about the place. The little home she took such pride in had deteriorated, thought Kerry sadly. A few months ago it had been spotless, every surface gleaming and the brasses round the fireplace twinkling. Now there were bundles of local papers and magazines littering the floor. The many photographs of Nellie's scattered family were filmed with dust and there were dead flies on the windowsills and plates of uneaten food on the table in the living room. It was a picture of decline Kerry had seen before in some of her elderly infirm patients whose relations lived too far away to help. She would have to persuade Nellie somehow that the time had come to accept help.

The old lady was standing precariously by the door to her kitchen, clinging to the back of a bookcase. She had an old blanket wrapped round her shoulders and she looked pinched and cold. She turned round as Kerry entered, a frown crossing her face when she saw who it was.

'I thought that nurse said Dr O'Mara was coming today,' she said grumpily.

'I'm afraid Dr O'Mara's been in an accident and injured himself rather badly. I don't think he'll be back for a while.'

Nellie pursed her lips. 'The way he screeches through the village in that car of his it's a miracle he hasn't come to grief before.'

The old lady turned back to her chair and staggered slightly as she let go of her support. Kerry went swiftly over to her and guided her gently back to her seat.

'It's a bit cold in here, Nellie, you haven't got your

fire on,' she said, bending down and switching on the electric fire in the grate. 'How are you feeling?'

'Not bad…not bad. Just a bit chilled, like, but what can you expect with this weather? I've not seen so much rain for many years.'

Kerry nodded—she'd had to cross parts of the road near Nellie's that were awash with huge puddles, and even from here she could hear the river gushing as it flowed along the main village road.

'Perhaps it'll stop raining soon, it did look a little lighter over the hills,' she said brightly. 'Now, Nellie, have you had anything to eat or drink today?'

Nellie looked evasive. 'I was just about to get myself a little something.'

'A bowl of soup might warm you up—I can easily heat some in a saucepan—and before you say anything, it isn't too much trouble.'

Kerry smiled at the old lady persuasively and was rewarded by a flicker of interest in her eyes. 'Well, just to please you, like, a little bit in a cup would be grand.'

In a few minutes thin hands were clasped round the warm cup and Nellie was sipping the soup eagerly, a little colour returning to her pale cheeks. 'That's very nice, Doctor, but I could have got it myself, you know.'

'I know you could, Nellie, but I want you to have a little rest for a while. I don't think you've ever recovered your strength from that last infection.'

Nellie's eyes flashed rebelliously. 'I'm not going back into that hospital, whatever you say!'

Kerry patted her hand. 'I don't want you to, but I do want to get you some help, just for the time being. Someone who can bring you a little food every day

and perhaps do your washing, build you up a little—
otherwise you're going to end up in hospital anyway.'

Nellie's frail old face looked fiercely at Kerry for a
minute, then slowly her expression changed to one of
resignation and she nodded her head slowly. 'Perhaps
I am a bit run-down. If you could organise something,
then—just temporary, mind!'

She must be feeling pretty awful to capitulate like
that, thought Kerry. It was never easy to admit, after
years of independence, that the time had come to be
cared for.

'I'll see to it,' promised Kerry. 'In the meantime,
Liz Ferris will be popping in to see that you're OK.'

'That Liz Ferris,' grumbled Nellie. 'She's always
getting on at me to put more fires on and get more food
in. She must think I'm made of money!'

'Now, now, Nellie—she's only doing it for your own
good, you know. We're all very fond of you and want
you to get stronger.'

Nellie looked slightly mollified. 'I know, lass, I
know.' She took another sip of soup and then looked
up at Kerry inquisitively. 'So what will you do now
without Dr O'Mara?'

'Oh, I'm sure I can get someone to fill in fairly
soon,' said Kerry, with more assurance than she felt.
She'd already been in touch with several agencies in
the area with no luck.

'I knew Frank O'Mara when he was a little boy—
him and his brother. I used to do some cooking for
them,' said Nellie, taking another sip of soup. 'Ee, they
were chalk and cheese, those lads. And wild—always
at each other's throats! Of course,' the old lady remi-
nisced, 'that father of theirs was hard on them, and

after he lost his first wife and his second wife left them all so sudden, like—well, they were left to their own devices and they were right tearaways!'

'I hope they've got over their differences now. His brother's coming up this afternoon to see Dr Frank,' said Kerry.

Nellie gave a cackle of laughter. 'Well, you may get fireworks between them—their father was a difficult, womanising man—perhaps they've taken after him! I always wondered if that was why Denovan's mother left—she was only young herself. But it was a cruel thing, if you ask me, to leave a young lad like that. You'll have to act as referee between them, my dear!'

That's the last thing I'm going to do, thought Kerry as she left the cottage. *I shall stay well clear of both of them.* She had enough on her plate without keeping the peace between two grown men! She had to admit, however, that the unexpected revelation Nellie had given about the O'Mara boys' childhood was rather intriguing. It sounded as if their childhood had not been a happy one.

She drove back to the surgery. The rain still beating down remorselessly—she wasn't surprised that the small car park was covered in huge puddles. A red sports car had taken the only dry slot near the staff spaces, so that Kerry had to park awkwardly against a wall and squeeze out of her door, putting her feet into a small pothole filled with water. She opened the boot and took out a large file and her medical bag, holding them in both arms as she picked her way over the flooded car park, the rain lashing down onto her and soaking her hair and clothes.

She squelched crossly into the building, hoping she

could dry her feet out before the late afternoon surgery. Surely the day couldn't get any worse! No happy holiday, just continual rain and cold and the prospect of weeks of hard work. Burdened by the things she was carrying, she opened the office door by pushing it with her back and going in backwards.

'Some stupid idiot's put their car in the only dry space,' she complained to the office at large. 'My feet are absolutely soaked.'

She dropped her files and bag on a chair and then a deep voice behind her made her whirl round.

'Ah—I'm sorry about that. It's my car taking the space. I'm afraid I didn't realise it was the only dry spot.'

A tall man with tousled dark hair who had been lounging against the side of the desk unravelled himself and stood up. His gaze swept slowly over Kerry's drenched figure and the dripping tendrils of hair plastered against her face, down to the soggy remnants of her shoes. Beside him, a small boy of about four years old, with a snub nose and round wire-rimmed glasses, sat on the desk, drumming his heels against the drawers.

'You're certainly very wet,' he murmured.

Tell me something I don't know, thought Kerry caustically, but she managed to disguise her irritation.

'You must be Denovan, Frank's brother,' she observed. 'I didn't think you'd be as early as this.' She looked at the small boy, now making little indentations with a pencil on the top of the desk. 'And this is?'

'This is Archie, my son,' explained Denovan. 'I had to bring him up with me as his nursery school closes in the afternoon and his childminder isn't well.' He smiled down at the child, and suddenly his stern face was softer, gentler. 'I couldn't leave you behind, could I, sweetheart?'

There was no mistaking the resemblance between the two—Archie was a miniature version of the man. She'd never heard Frank mention that Denovan had a child, or indeed of him having a partner. What an odd family they were. Kerry wondered where Archie's mother was—perhaps she had a high-powered job that meant she wasn't around in the evening?

Denovan O'Mara was taller and broader than she'd thought he'd be—in fact, the television screen didn't do him justice. He was one hot guy, over six feet of impressive bodywork and a strong no-nonsense face— firm lips, incredibly blue bright eyes. He was impeccably dressed in a dark blue suit with a crisply knotted tie. No wonder he'd fitted so easily into celebrity status. Central casting couldn't have done better!

She caught an alarming glimpse of her own appearance in the mirror over the basin—hair hanging like rats' tails over her face, slightly blurred eye makeup…for some reason it irked her that she looked such a wreck in front of Denovan O'Mara and his smooth appearance.

She opened a drawer in the desk and took out a small towel, drying her face and hands vigorously. 'You must have set off quite early from London,' she said.

'I came straight from work this morning—I told you I'd come as soon as I could,' he said. 'I've only a very limited amount of time here, but I thought I'd pop into your surgery first to tell you I'd arrived.' He shook her hand in a firm grip, his vivid blue eyes holding hers.

'You'll be pleased to hear that they've stabilised

Frank—although he's still in ICU,' Kerry informed him, then added with slight emphasis to ensure that Denovan realised just how ill Frank was, 'I think it was pretty touch-and-go last night.'

He nodded. 'Sounds as if he was lucky to get out alive. But he's a strong man—he'll pull through, no doubt,' he said in an offhand way. His glance swept over her keenly, noting the dark shadows under her eyes, the strain showing on her face. 'This can't be easy for you,' he observed. 'I suppose you're trying to organise a locum and a hundred other things as well? You look a little bushed.'

For a 'little bushed' read a 'complete wreck', she thought wryly, blinking in some surprise at his understanding of the situation. She nodded briefly—there was something about his sympathetic tone that undermined her previous impression of a self-centred man. No wonder he held thousands of women viewers under his spell—not only looks, but reasonably charming when he wanted to be, as well. In fact, she could see that some women would find his type of looks quite sexy! But again, Frank knew his brother better than she did and she could quite believe his remarks that Denovan had an inflated idea of his own importance.

The small boy put his face close to his father's. 'I'm hungry,' he pronounced. 'I need a biscuit!'

'You wait until we get to the pub where we're going to stay then you can have lots to eat,' his father promised.

Archie pulled his father's ear. 'I can't wait.' He raised his voice. 'I'm very hungry!'

'I don't know if Daphne's rung up the Pear Tree yet—your room probably won't be ready,' said Kerry.

'I've had bad news on that front.' Daphne came into the room, catching the end of the sentence. 'The drains can't cope with the extra water at the bottom of the hill and the pub's completely flooded—they've had to close it and there's nowhere else to stay for miles.'

'Oh, no!' Kerry looked in dismay first at Daphne and then at Denovan and Archie. 'If the pub's flooded, what about all the other buildings down there?' And even more urgently, she thought worriedly, where was this man and his little boy going to stay?

'I'm *really* hungry, Daddy,' growled Archie, looking angrily at his father. 'Please can I have a biscuit, quickly? You promised before!'

Kerry couldn't help smiling at the little boy. She could imagine where he got his impatience from! 'Daphne, you've met Frank's brother already, I think?'

Daphne dimpled at Denovan, clearly smitten. 'Only a few minutes ago. Look, why don't I give Archie something nice to eat from the kitchen?' She held out her hand to Archie. 'You come with me, pet.'

Archie slid down from the desk and ran across the room to Daphne.

Denovan smiled wryly. 'Looks like he's got a friend there. It's a nuisance about the hotel. I guess I'll have to drive back to London after I've seen Frank this evening.'

Kerry had a spare room in her little cottage. It was filled with junk, but it did have a bed in it, and it would only be for one night after all. It was a nuisance, but for Archie's sake she would have to offer the arrogant Denovan and his son a room for the night.

'You're very welcome to stay with me,' she said, without much enthusiasm. 'I've a sleeping bag that Archie could have, and…' she looked doubtfully at Denovan's large frame '…a single bed in my spare room—it might not be very comfortable.'

There was a surprising sweetness in the smile that lifted his stern face. It made him seem younger, more approachable.

'That's very kind. I don't really feel like making the journey back tonight.' His periwinkle eyes smiled engagingly at her. They were quite startling, those eyes of his. 'I'm sorry to impose on you. I feel I've put you out enough, but I promise we'll be very quiet guests.'

'No, that's fine, it's no trouble.'

'Well, we'll be out of your hair tomorrow anyway, but I'm very grateful to have somewhere to sleep tonight!'

'That's OK,' she said brusquely. She delved in her bag and brought out her house keys, tossing them to him. 'You might as well go there now and get settled. There's food in the fridge for you and Archie. The house is at the top of the hill beyond the surgery—you can't miss it, it's the only one with a blue door.'

Denovan jingled the keys in his hand before he turned to go, with a slightly apologetic expression on his face. 'Actually, I have another very big favour to ask you. I'll go and see Frank this evening—but an ICU isn't the place for a little boy, and I was planning to ask one of the hotel staff to watch him for me, but that plan will obviously need to change. So, if you're not doing anything tonight, could I possibly leave Archie with you for an hour?'

Not doing anything tonight? Kerry almost laughed. She only had about a hundred things on her to-do list from the fallout of Frank's accident, like sorting out the paperwork she should have done last night, trying yet again to get some cover for her colleague, catching up on the seriously ill patients on his list. It seemed an endless catalogue of things. But Denovan had to see his brother and Archie had to be looked after.

She hid her sigh behind a smile. 'No problem—I'll be back after surgery at about six-thirty.'

'I'm very grateful. I just want to satisfy myself they're doing the best they can for him. Then I really have to get back to London early tomorrow. Archie needs to get back to his nursery school.'

'Of course.'

'I don't know when I can get back here again, it rather depends on my other commitments. As I said before, Frank's accident couldn't have come at a worse time.'

Kerry thought of poor Frank lying so very injured in the local hospital, and raised her eyebrows. Denovan watched her expression.

'You look very disapproving,' he remarked, a sudden coolness in his tone. 'I do have an incredibly busy life, and it's been a nightmare trying to rearrange things today, but I managed it.'

Bully for you, thought Kerry scornfully, but she said lightly, 'I guess I'm just a little surprised that you couldn't have found time to come at the weekend perhaps. I'd have thought…'

The blue eyes turned flinty. 'You'd have thought what exactly?' he enquired frostily. 'With the deepest respect, you have no right to presume anything about my arrangements.'

Talk about pompous! Kerry's cheeks burned angrily. 'I don't presume anything—and it hasn't been easy for me either, as a matter of fact, but if he was my brother—'

'But he's not!' cut in Denovan harshly.

Kerry stared at him incredulously, astounded by his rudeness. Extraordinary how touchy and defensive he was about visiting his brother, it was as if she'd lit a blue touch paper! She felt she'd glimpsed the real Denovan O'Mara again, arrogant and self-centred, and all of a sudden the atmosphere in the room had dropped several degrees.

Denovan stared at the floor for a second, taking a deep breath as if trying to keep his anger under control, then he shook his head apologetically and looked slightly shamefaced.

'Look, I'm sorry. I didn't mean to fly off the handle. It was completely uncalled for, especially when you've been so kind.'

Hah! thought Kerry cynically. Now she was seeing his charming TV persona once more.

'I guess it's been a hell of a long day,' Denovan continued. 'I just wish Frank could learn not to take liberties with his blasted car.'

Amen to that, agreed Kerry. Frank wasn't aware of the upset he'd caused her over the past twenty-four hours!

'Perhaps he's learned his lesson,' observed Kerry tersely. 'However, I'm sure when he sees you, it will do him a lot of good.'

Denovan shrugged. 'Actually, it could have quite the opposite effect. The last time I saw or spoke to Frank was over six years ago, and that wasn't exactly a happy occasion.' He said it lightly, but that only seemed to emphasise the gravity of their differences.

* * *

He turned and left the room, striding quickly down the corridor and attempting to gather his thoughts. God, he was a fool. Why had he flown off the handle when Kerry had queried his commitment to his brother? All she had done was express sympathy and offer hospitality to himself and Archie—and he'd repaid her by being incredibly rude.

The truth was, he admitted to himself, he had a terrible fear that coming back and seeing Frank would raise all kinds of ghosts that he'd tried to bury over the years—and perhaps there was some guilt that he had never attempted to build bridges with his brother.

Of course, Kerry knew nothing of the terrible legacy of betrayal and disgust he felt for Frank, and the bitterness that had grown up between the two men. He clenched his fists angrily. Hell, he didn't owe his brother any sympathy at all after what he'd done to ruin the family. He took a deep breath and went to collect his little boy from the kitchen.

Kerry sat down and stared after him in astonishment. What earth-shattering event could have caused a six-year rift between the two brothers? And whatever it was, did it justify Denovan's rudeness?

CHAPTER TWO

ARCHIE settled happily in front of the television while his father went to see Frank in the local hospital, which was about five miles away across the valley in the larger town of Laystone. Denovan said he would probably stay an hour and find out what the prognosis on Frank was.

Kerry put on the kettle and started to make a quick supper for herself and Archie. She flicked a look at the little boy, endearingly quaint with his round glasses perched on the end of his snub nose, his jaws moving rhythmically as he devoured a little bowl of raisins. He seemed an adaptable child—obviously well used to adjusting to new people and situations.

'Would you like some pasta?' she enquired.

He didn't take his eyes from the screen. 'No, I don't like pasta, thank you.'

'What about some baked beans, then?' Kerry rooted around in a cupboard looking for suitable food.

'No, I don't like baked beans, thank you.'

'Then what do you like?'

Archie dragged himself away from watching the flickering screen. 'I like chips and burgers and ice cream and crisps and chocolate,' he said firmly.

Kerry's lips twitched in amusement—evidently his parents didn't bother about healthy diets!

'Is that what you're allowed at home?'

Archie fixed Kerry with his bright blue eyes and nodded vigorously. 'Yes. Daddy says I can have what I want.'

'Right, well, I'll see what I can find,' she promised, wondering where Mummy fitted into the picture.

A few minutes later Kerry collapsed on the sofa next to Archie and tucked into her pasta, giving the little boy some ice cream she'd found at the bottom of the freezer, and both of them sat in silence, one absorbed in the television, Kerry starting to look through her mail and flicking through the newspaper she hadn't had time to read that day.

The room was warm and she fought against drifting off to sleep—it had been a hectic twenty-four hours, and she was feeling the effects of cramming a lot of things into a short time with little sleep. Archie leant cosily against her like a little hot-water bottle and she looked down at the top of his head. He was such a lovable little boy, even if his father was the arrogant Dr Denovan O'Mara!

She sighed softly. A year ago her future had seemed to be mapped out—a wedding, a loving husband, hope-fully followed by children like Archie... Then all that had been taken away from her brutally and swiftly, and the children and family life she longed for were noth-ing but a faded dream.

She was vaguely aware of the sound of the front door opening just as she closed her eyes in a troubled doze. Denovan walked into the room then stopped sud-denly when he saw his son and Kerry relaxed together on the sofa. Archie had his head against her shoulder, and Kerry had one arm round him, her freshly washed dark cloud of hair tumbling over the cushion she was leaning against, mouth slightly open as she dozed. He smiled wistfully at the picture they presented—it twisted his heart to see Archie nestled up against Kerry, for it seemed to highlight the lack of a motherly figure in his precious son's life.

He sighed and pushed that thought to the back of his mind then leant forward and touched Kerry lightly on her shoulder. 'Sorry to disturb you when you both seem so comfortable,' he said.

Startled, Kerry sat bolt upright on the sofa and stared at him in surprise. 'You've hardly been gone any time!' she exclaimed.

'I haven't been able to get to the hospital,' Denovan explained drily. 'The wind's brought down several big trees by the riverbank and the bridge has collapsed—there's no way over the river now, so getting anywhere out of the village at the moment is impossible. It won't take much for the river to burst its banks completely.'

'What?' Kerry gently put Archie to one side and stood up, staring in disbelief at Denovan. 'The village is cut off altogether? So what's happening down by the river now?'

He shook his head. 'People are working like mad, putting sandbags or anything else round their properties to keep the water out. But the most immediate problem is that a woman's trapped under part of the bridge wall that's collapsed.' His face was grave. 'I'm sorry to say I'll have to drag you away. We're both needed urgently, and this woman needs medical help. There's no way an ambulance can get through at the moment. There are people trying to free her, but she's bound to have injuries—we should be there.'

The day she'd thought could get no worse had reached rock bottom, thought Kerry wryly. A disaster in the village and no backup from essential services. Kerry hauled on her cagoule and pushed her feet into some wellingtons—she flicked a look at Denovan's stalwart figure and suddenly she was extremely grateful to have him with her to help, pompous and arrogant man though he was.

'We'd better take my car,' she said. 'It's a small estate so we could get her up to the surgery in that if necessary. We keep some equipment there for the Mountain Rescue Team—a stretcher, a collapsible splint, blankets and a neck collar, that sort of thing. We can call in and get them.'

'A good idea,' said Denovan. 'It's very cold out there.'

Kerry noticed the little boy looking solemnly at them both. 'We'll drop Archie off at Daphne's—she's only a door or two away and I know she won't mind.' She bent down and smiled at him. 'You know that nice lady who gave you biscuits and hot milk this afternoon? We're taking you to stay with her for an hour or two while your daddy and I go and help a poorly lady.'

Archie's mischievous blue eyes gleamed. 'Will she give me some more biscuits?'

'I dare say she will.' Kerry smiled. 'Come on, let's go!'

A small crowd had gathered round the bridge where the river started to run through the village. Car headlights were trained on the dramatic scene where the woman lay trapped, with her legs pinioned underneath the collapsed stones. The lashing rain glinted on a million drops in the beams of the light, and the river looked very full; it was obvious that the bridge had been swept away.

Kerry's eyes widened in horror as the enormity of the situation hit her. 'Oh, my God,' she breathed, scrambling out of the car. 'How on earth will we get her out without equipment?'

Denovan opened the car tailgate and lifted out the blankets. 'We'll do it somehow,' he said confidently. 'You'd be surprised what a few strong men can do.' He gave her a quick grin of encouragement. 'You keep the lady calm and assess her condition and I'll help these men to lift that rubble.'

Kerry turned to a woman on the edge of the little crowd. 'Have you any idea who's under all that rubble?' she asked.

'She's Sirie Patel. She runs the Post Office and shop on the corner, poor woman. She never stops working—if it wasn't for her, we wouldn't have a village shop.'

Kerry pushed her way through to the stricken woman, forcing herself into professional mode and forgetting her own shock that it was her friend Sirie who was hurt. She didn't deserve this, giving so much of her life to the community, allowing those who were hard up to pay her 'next time', lending a ready ear to listen to the woes of any of her customers. It wasn't fair.

In her next life, thought Kerry grimly as she packed the blankets as best she could around Sirie in the howling wind and stinging rain, she would come back as something less stressful than a GP trying to calm a terrified woman trapped under a bridge wall with water gushing over her. Perhaps she'd have a career as a lion tamer or a high-flying trapeze artist!

She pushed a folded blanket gently behind Sirie's head, all the time talking to her, reassuring her that she was being looked after. Kerry knew the psychological importance of making sure the victim was aware that she wasn't alone but in safe and capable hands.

'It's all right, Sirie, love, we're here to help you now,' shouted Kerry above the noise of the rushing river. 'Try and stay calm. Here, hold my hand and grip it tightly. If you keep as still as possible, there's going to be no danger.'

Oh, how she hoped that was true! The river was so very close and fast, the roar of it filling their ears. She had a horrible vision that if Sirie were to slip into it when they released her, she could be swept down into the torrent. It was a steep hill, and even though it was raining and dark, the ribbon of lights along the road at the bottom of the valley could be seen clearly, twinkling many feet below.

Kerry looked across at Denovan lying on his stomach close to Sirie as he tried to see where her legs were trapped, and if the two large slabs of stone were actually compressing the limbs. She admitted to herself that she hadn't expected a man like Denovan to hurl himself into the situation as he had—to be so hands-on. He'd surprised her, but after the way he'd lost his cool with her earlier, she wasn't about to become his biggest fan. However, she admitted grudgingly, she was very grateful that he was there, and revealing himself to be so competent.

He scrambled up and crouched near to Kerry, his

eyes looking searchingly at the victim's face. 'How is Sirie?' he asked. 'Bearing up?'

'Very shocked. She's in considerable pain, and her pulse is quite thready—of course I don't know what her sats are or her BP. I've morphine in my bag so perhaps you'd dig it out. Any sign of outside help yet?'

'I've rung for an air ambulance, seeing nothing else can get through here at the moment,' said Denovan, rummaging through Kerry's bag to find the morphine. 'The reception was incredibly bad, but I think they've got the gist of it. It sounded like a ten-minute ETA.'

Sirie's grip on Kerry's hand was fierce. 'Will they be long getting me out?' she whispered, screwing her eyes up. 'I don't know how long I can stand this…'

'It's all right, Sirie, you're going to feel more comfortable very soon. Dr O'Mara's just going to inject you with something that'll make you feel much easier.' Sirie's eyes fluttered open. 'What about my girls?' she whispered. 'I've got to pick them up from their Brownie meeting.'

'Don't worry. We'll make sure that they're looked after. One of the mothers will take them to her house,' Kerry assured her. Thank heavens for a small, close-knit community, she thought. They did look out for each other here.

Denovan tested the syringe he was holding, then smiled down at Sirie. 'Hang in there. Ten mils of this magic stuff will help you to relax. In fact, you'll feel on top of the world, as if you've had two double whiskies…'

Sirie's face flickered into a frail, brave smile. 'I'm teetotal, Doctor,' she whispered. 'I never touch the stuff!'

'Well, now you're about to find out what you're missing,' he joked. He turned to Kerry, his voice low enough so that Sirie couldn't hear him but audible to Kerry above the noise of the voices of the men and the howling wind. 'We're nearly there now. Keep your fingers crossed.'

Kerry bit her lip, watching the last stones being inched away from Sirie's legs, praying that the muscles in the legs wouldn't be badly crushed. Whatever damage Sirie had suffered, it was imperative that she was hospitalised as soon as possible.

She watched the men grunting and groaning as they tried to lever the stones up without slipping in the thick mud around the site. Denovan and two other men had placed the stretcher on the ground as near to the bridge as possible and were waiting to pull the victim out as soon as they dared. It was a tense few minutes and Kerry kept up a low flow of conversation with Sirie, distracting her from the shouting and noise of falling rubble that was going on around her.

At last, with infinite care, Sirie was lifted away from the broken bridge and placed as gently as possibly on the stretcher. Kerry and Denovan bent over her to examine the damage that had been done to her legs. One lay awkwardly, bent at a strange angle with multiple contusions and a large gash down the shin bone.

'We might have guessed Sirie wouldn't get away without any injury,' said Denovan, straightening up. 'That left leg's almost certainly broken, from the way it's positioned. It's taken the brunt of the fallen wall, but I don't see a protruding bone, so hopefully it's not a compound fracture.'

Kerry squeezed Sirie's hand comfortingly, and Sirie's large, scared eyes looked from one doctor to the other. 'Am I going to have to have an operation?' she asked in a quavery voice.

'Until you've had X-rays we won't know for sure. First thing we need to get you to hospital.' Denovan squatted down next to the frightened woman and smiled kindly at her. 'You've been absolutely great—really brave. Just hang on a little longer.'

Kerry was amazed at how sensitive Denovan could be, what a contrast to the impatient doctor of an hour or two ago. He seemed to have another, softer side to him that he'd hidden well when she'd first met him—perhaps he was just very good at acting!

He was looking at the raging river a few feet away from them. 'Perhaps we'll move Sirie nearer the car first and then strap her leg.'

Kerry followed his glance and swallowed hard. Was it her imagination, or did the water seem higher than it had been? It looked as if the river would burst its banks any second and completely cover the road.

'OK, Doc, but let's do it before the whole damn things goes,' urged one of the men. 'Hopefully the helicopter will be here soon. It'll land on the field at the top of the village.' They slid the stretcher into the back of the estate car, although it wouldn't go in completely, and Kerry bound the affected leg above the site of the fracture to the splint—just securing it enough to stop it from being bounced around. Four men, including Denovan, supported the stretcher as Kerry drove very slowly back through the village to The Larches. As she left the scene, she heard a sudden commotion behind her—a roar of water, the cracking of trees.

'What's happening back there?' she shouted, keeping her eyes glued ahead of her.

'The river's burst its banks—we got Sirie out just in time,' yelled one of the men.

Oh, the relief when the little entourage eventually reached the medical centre—three stalwart figures in familiar orange and green emergency suits were racing down the road to meet them.

'We've managed to land in the field at the top of the road,' panted one of the paramedics. 'You did well to get this lady out when you did. I believe the river's completely out of control now. We'll just do an assessment of the victim before we move her any farther—get a take on her oxygen levels, BP, etc.'

Kerry leant against the car and watched Sirie being monitored by the medics. If the men in the village hadn't managed to free her so quickly, there might have been a tragic end to the story, she thought with a shudder. She glanced across at Denovan, who was talking to one of the paramedics and watching as they assessed Sirie's condition.

'Can you get word through to the other emergency services that the village needs help?' he asked one of the paramedics. 'My mobile's not getting through to anyone at the moment and someone's just told me some power lines are down.'

Sirie was eventually taken away, wrapped in a foil heat blanket to keep her body temperature up, and soon the clatter of the helicopter's rotor blades were heard as it rose in the air and headed off across the valley. Kerry brushed a weary hand of relief over her eyes—what a way to finish the last twenty-four hours! Adrenaline had been pumping through her for the last hour, but suddenly the drama was over and she felt drained of all her energy.

'Tired?' asked Denovan, his eyes looking critically at her exhausted-looking face.

'A little,' she admitted, then added with sudden candour, 'Actually, I feel I could go to sleep on a clothesline for three days after all that's happened. I'm going to leave the car here, I think, as I thought I heard something important give a horrible crack as we set off with Sirie, but I'll look at it in the morning.'

'You need a hot drink,' he ordered, mock-severely. 'And perhaps something a little stronger, if you've got anything in. Come on, I'll walk you to your house before I pick up Archie.'

'You've no need to,' protested Kerry firmly. 'It's late. You go and get Archie now.' She wasn't about to get too chummy with an unpredictable man like Denovan just because he'd helped out so much that evening. She was still smarting at the conversation she'd had with him earlier.

'Your house is on the way to Daphne's so I might as well see you back first,' he said easily.

They went up the hill together silently, heads down against the wind. In the dark it was hard to see the path, and although Kerry moved cautiously, the pothole she stepped into took her by surprise. Suddenly she sensed the ground coming towards her face and flailed her arms to keep her balance and stop her smashing against the asphalt of the path.

In an instant Denovan's arms were round her waist, pulling her towards him. 'Steady does it,' he murmured.

She gasped in surprise, momentarily winded, and

for a second she clung on to him, dazed at the speed
of it all, braced against his rocklike frame. Feeling the
rough texture of his chin stubble rasping against the
softness of her face, and the cold damp clothes he was
wearing pressed against hers somehow seemed embar-
rassingly intimate with someone she didn't know—but
nevertheless she leaned into him, prolonging the contact, relaxing as she savoured that sensation of protec-
tion, the physical strength of him. And unexpectedly
for an extraordinary moment she felt the unmistakeable
flicker of physical attraction for Denovan O'Mara, a
man she'd instinctively disliked since she'd spoken to
him on the phone that morning.

A poignant memory of being in another man's arms
floated into her mind, and in her imagination she was
close to Andy again, so close that she could feel the
thump of his heart against hers, enclosed in the warmth
and safety of the man she'd loved so much only twelve
months ago. But how long ago that seemed now, another life away...

Then the wind blew cold against her face and she
was back in the present, and to her embarrassment
tears welled up in her eyes. Her grief for Andy was still
very near the surface, and she felt a funny little shiver
of guilt, as if she'd betrayed his memory. She stepped
back from Denovan hastily, almost shoving him away
from her, and gave a nervous laugh.

'I'm so clumsy...'

'It's pitch dark—no wonder you lost your footing.
Are you OK?' he asked, his hand taking her arm in
an iron grip again. 'We don't want another casualty,
do we?'

He looked down into her eyes, his own glinting with

amusement, rivulets of water running down his face, his teeth white in the shadows, the lean planes of his muddied scratched face showing up every so often in the headlights of the cars coming up the hill and away from the flooding.

There was no doubt about it—he was a very attractive man. Kerry's heart did a stealthy double beat and the treacherous flicker of attraction flashed through her again, and to her shame in her imagination she pictured herself kissing this man, feeling his firm mouth on hers, his cheek against hers. Then she looked away, sick at heart. How could she fancy another man so quickly? It was Andy she wanted, missed so desperately, and no one could fill the gap he'd left. What on earth was she thinking of—allowing herself to imagine anything intimate with a man she didn't even like?

'I'm absolutely fine,' she said distantly. 'Just lost my footing for a second.'

'Lucky I'm here, then, isn't it?' he murmured, his hand still holding her arm as they went into the warm little cottage.

He flicked on the light switch. 'A miracle,' he remarked. 'The power's still on.' He looked at Kerry's white face and said sternly, 'You need some sleep. Get up to your bedroom, and I'll bring you a hot drink when you're actually in bed.'

Denovan looked pretty tired, as well. His face was covered with mud, as was his hitherto immaculately tailored suit—the trousers were ripped and the sleeves of the jacket almost torn away from their seams. But it was his hands that Kerry noticed with horror—torn, bleeding, the nails jagged—they had been badly damaged in the race to free Sirie.

'Oh, Denovan, your poor hands!' She forgot that she disliked the man and without thinking took his hands in hers and looked down at them in distress. 'You've got to get these cleaned as they're very badly cut. There's disinfectant in the bathroom cupboards.'

He pulled them gently away from her. 'Don't worry, Doctor, they'll be OK. It's just a few surface abrasions.'

Kerry bit her lip. Why had she done something so personal as holding his hand? It implied a degree of intimacy with him that she certainly didn't feel.

He said briskly, 'Now, I'm going to make you some hot cocoa with a nip of whisky in it. It'll do you a world of good.'

Kerry didn't argue, too tired to dwell on her embarrassment at holding his hands, but stumbled into her room, not even bothering to pull off her clothes. She collapsed onto the heavenly soft bed in her filthy clothes, and as soon as her head hit the pillow her eyes closed, and she never heard Denovan come upstairs with a mug of cocoa.

Denovan put the mug on the side table and smiled down at her wryly. No wonder the woman was exhausted—she'd had a lot to cope with since the night before. For a few seconds he looked at her recumbent slim figure, her tangled dark hair spread across the pillow, long eyelashes sweeping over her high cheekbones. Those delicate looks belied the toughness she'd shown tonight in the raging storm, he reflected.

He grinned, forgetting for a moment how tired he was. It was hard to believe that a few minutes ago he'd held this beautiful woman in his arms, felt her soft body pressed to his—and very nice it had been, too! And hadn't it reminded him very forcibly that despite

the so-called glamorous social whirl he was supposed
to enjoy, he'd led a pretty monastic life over the past
few years despite his years in the limelight and being
featured with nearly every glamorous young woman in
London? Since Archie's mother had left he was wary
of being linked to any one woman. And anyway, he
had to be very choosy—whoever he took up with had
to be very, very special, someone who would cher-
ish his little boy as much as he did. And, he thought
sadly, show more affection for Archie than his own
mother ever had.

He supposed that someone like Kerry would have
a boyfriend. Obviously she wasn't married, but she
was an attractive and successful woman. Fleetingly he
wondered how she could work with a bastard like his
brother—but he guessed that Kerry was pretty feisty
and she wouldn't suffer fools gladly. Or perhaps it was
more likely, Denovan thought cynically, that his brother
had hidden his true character from her. After all, that
was Frank's stock in trade—pretending to be something he wasn't.

Gently he placed the duvet over her and turned to
go out of the room, nearly falling over a large suitcase
with a folded dress draped on top of it by the door.
He bent down to look at the labels and raised his eyebrows. It looked like Kerry was, or had been, going on
holiday—Frank's stupid accident had obviously meant
that she'd had to forfeit that. No wonder she'd been a
bit tetchy with him. Her plans had been ruined and instead of a fairy-tale holiday she was back at work for
a long stint if Frank's injuries were as serious as they
thought they were.

He went down to the little kitchen and stretched before flopping down in a chair, his elbows on the table, and closed his eyes for a second. Although he felt exhausted, he had decisions to make before he returned to London. His contract with the television company was ending, but the company wanted him to front another programme about the general health of the population, and he was wondering whether he really wanted to take on more work. Wondering, in fact, if he actually wanted to do any more television work at all.

On the face of it, his life had all seemed so glamorous and exciting, working in a place with a buzz to it, mingling with the good and the great, knowing that he had a certain cachet amongst his colleagues. But the truth was he was bored with answering people's queries and giving his opinion on hypothetical questions—and the boredom was beginning to show. He was easily irritated, becoming autocratic if someone didn't agree with him, used to having his own way.

Tonight had made him realise that he was becoming further and further removed from the practical care of the patients he'd loved treating. He'd just been thrown into a situation a few hours ago where he'd used the skills he'd been taught at medical school and as a result he felt alive, stimulated, his body humming with the unaccustomed rush of adrenaline. It had been so rewarding to help in Sirie's rescue, working in a team and establishing a relationship with the victim, persuading her to put her trust in himself and Kerry. It had been worthwhile—and how long had it been since he'd felt like that at the end of a day's work? A few years ago he'd have given anything to achieve what he had done in the media world, but suddenly it was beginning to seem a very hollow world.

He rose restlessly from his chair, went to the back door and opened it. The wind had died down and it had stopped raining, and there was a sweet country-fresh smell from the fields. He took a deep gulp of the crisp air into his lungs; he'd forgotten how much he'd loved Braxton Falls, the little valleys and the rolling hills. It had been the best part of his childhood, growing up in the countryside. He hadn't realised how much he'd missed it since he'd left six years ago after falling out so spectacularly with Frank. His father had wanted them both to take over the practice when he retired— but Denovan had known that working with his half-brother was an impossibility. After what had happened, they could never live near each other again, and so he'd ended up in London and his life had taken a very different direction from anything he'd imagined.

He closed the door and turned back abruptly into the room. He would have to go and collect Archie from Daphne's house, and then tomorrow start thinking seriously about his future, because it wasn't just his future that was affected but his dear little son's—and he was the most important thing of all.

CHAPTER THREE

SHE couldn't understand where the voices were coming from… Kerry stirred restlessly as she slowly awoke and a child's high little voice floated upstairs, singing 'Humpty Dumpty', penetrating her sleepy brain. And then there was a burst of giggling, a clattering of kitchen noises, and someone running a tap.

She squinted across at her bedside clock, then as it came into focus gave a yelp of horror—it was nine o'clock and she should have been at work an hour ago! She saw the still-full mug of cold cocoa on the table and everything came flooding back—Frank's accident, the drama last night, and the bursting of the riverbank. So many things had happened yesterday. She'd almost forgotten that Denovan and his son were staying with her.

Denovan O'Mara. She rolled on her back and closed her eyes and like the rerun of a film a picture floated into her mind of her falling forward and being swept up in his arms. She could still feel the shiver of attraction that had flickered through her body and how it had shaken her. Oh, sure, he was the kind of drop-dead gorgeous male that most girls would die for—but not her. She had fallen in love with Andy, sweet, gentle, self-effacing and kind. She'd never been attracted to

Denovan's assured, smooth type—especially when it was mixed with arrogance!

OK, she'd been grateful for his undoubted skill last night, and he'd certainly thrown himself into the rescue. He'd actually been rather heroic, she admitted, battling against the weather as he'd helped to dismantle the fallen wall, directing the team of men, putting himself at risk when he'd helped to lift Sirie over the mud near the raging river. And perhaps it was her admiration for his contribution last night that had made her act in such an odd way—yes, that had to be it. And anyway, and most importantly, Denovan O'Mara was obviously a family man with a child—however attractive, he was off-limits!

She swung her legs over the bed and started to peel off her filthy clothes from the night before. She drew back the curtains and looked down the street, amazed that, instead of rain, sunlight bathed the village in a golden light and the hills beyond had a backdrop of blue skies. It was hard to believe that there'd been a raging storm that night. Still, the road was covered with thick mud and she could see knots of people making their way up the hill from the flooded road below. Abandoned cars were strewn haphazardly on pavements and across the road. She was profoundly glad that Denovan and his son were only staying for the one night and would be going today—she had enough problems to worry about without catering for two guests.

A quick shower and a change of clothes and Kerry made her way downstairs, a delicious smell of fresh coffee permeating the little cottage. It reminded her that it had been a long, long time since she'd had anything to eat or drink and a cup of hot coffee would revive her more than anything else. Straight afterwards she'd ring the surgery and tell them she'd be along directly. She imagined the bulging roomful of patients waiting to see her, and sighed. How the hell would she ever get through them all?

In the kitchen Denovan was on his mobile phone, his back to her, and Archie was sitting at the kitchen table, consuming a pile of toast. He gazed at Kerry and smiled.

'Here's that lady again,' he informed his father. 'She's got out of bed now.'

Kerry pulled the coffee pot towards her and poured out a large mug of coffee. 'Hello, Archie, did you have a good sleep?'

The little boy nodded solemnly. 'But Daddy didn't. He kept falling out of that bed. It's too small for him.'

Denovan snapped his mobile shut and turned round with a grin. 'Hey, I was very grateful for that bed, young man.' He looked at Kerry. 'You went out like a light—I'm not surprised.'

The ruined suit had gone and now he was wearing jeans and an old fisherman's jersey, and although his hair had been washed, as it had dried it had sprung up in a tousled way over his forehead—he looked very casual and it suited him. Kerry pinched a piece of toast from Archie's plate.

'What's been happening? What about the village—I suppose they've managed to open up the road?'

Denovan shook his head. 'No bridge, no road, some power lines down—and a lot of houses with flooding. No way out or into the village, and now I was just hearing there may be a problem with the helicopter. By the way, I went down to the surgery and told them you'd be a little late.' His eyes twinkled. 'I think you're in for a busy morning.'

'I can imagine,' remarked Kerry wryly. 'How about your brother? Have you managed to contact the hospital?'

'Still stable—and Sirie Patel is having surgery this morning on her leg. There is evidence of crush syndrome, I'm afraid. Her kidney function seems impaired with all the toxins in her blood—but hopefully they've got it under control.'

So much had happened—so much to do. 'I'll get going, then,' said Kerry briskly. 'No good sitting around here.'

'I wondered can I be of any help?' suggested Denovan slightly tentatively. 'I don't want to step on anyone's toes, but if we could find some childcare for Archie for an hour or two, I could see some of your patients for you until they manage to open up the road.'

Kerry looked at him sardonically, and couldn't help enquiring rather pertly, 'I thought you had to get back to London—that it was very inconvenient to stay on?'

Touché, thought Denovan wryly. He deserved that dart of sarcasm! 'I won't be able to leave Braxton, with the roads as they are, and even if they do manage to get a helicopter through I doubt if I'll be a priority. I might as well make myself useful.'

Kerry's face softened—she'd be stupid to pass by the offer of help from someone she'd seen to be competent. 'You're sure? I have to admit it would be a great help. And perhaps by lunchtime they'll have repaired the bridge. And as for Archie—there's a little nursery school in the church hall just across the road. I'm sure in an emergency they'd look after him.'

They'd probably fall over themselves to look after the famous Denovan O'Mara's son, Kerry reflected with a little private grin to herself.

To Kerry's amazement, the church hall was milling with people, children ran round excitedly and some of the older men and women were sitting on benches by the wall looking disorientated and a little lost. A trestle table had been set up along one side of the room, where several women, including Daphne, were filling mugs with tea and coffee.

'What on earth's going on?' Kerry asked her.

'Everyone from down near the bridge has had to be evacuated. Some of these people came up here early in the morning to sleep because the water got so high in their houses. It's complete bedlam,' said Daphne.

'I suppose Freda's in charge at the surgery, then?' said Kerry resignedly.

Freda Knight was their trainee receptionist. She'd only recently left school but her grip on the job was precarious, as most of her life was lived vicariously through the pages of the gossip magazines and the celebrities in them, and she seemed to have little interest in the running of the surgery. Kerry wondered if Freda would be able to concentrate at all when she realised that Denovan O'Mara was going to be helping out!

'I'll be over very soon,' promised Daphne. 'We just felt we had to give some of these elderly folk something hot to drink.'

Kerry looked around the crowded room. 'I don't suppose the nursery school is operating today, then,' she said. 'Denovan's offered to help out with this morning's list and we were hoping we could leave Archie with them for an hour or so until he goes back later today.'

Daphne looked quizzically at Denovan. 'Unless your car has wings, I don't think you'll be going anywhere fast—they say the bridge will take days to repair. The army's down there now, but it's not looking good.'

'It doesn't matter.' He shrugged. 'They'll get someone else to step in and hold the fort for me no doubt. It's just Archie I'm concerned about.'

'I tell you what,' suggested Daphne. 'My three boys are in the hall right now and Archie got to know them last night. I know they'd be pleased to look after him for you. Larry's fifteen and reasonably sensible. School's been cancelled for today at least, so they can take him home and play with him. If they need you, you're only at the medical centre, which is practically opposite our house.'

Archie was already beaming up at his father. 'Jack's got a great big train with signals,' he said. 'He'll let me play with that!'

Daphne laughed. 'You've certainly got an easy son to deal with,' she said. 'You don't know how lucky you are.'

Denovan smiled and for a fleeting second his eyes met Kerry's. 'As long as he hasn't inherited the O'Mara temper—I wouldn't wish that on anyone!'

In the waiting room the patients looked tired and shocked after a terrible night of confusion. There was a low murmur of hushed conversation as they went over the awful events of the night. Many of their homes would have been ruined with the flooding and most of them would have had no sleep. Kerry wasn't surprised that some of them looked bruised and battered. She called out a cheery 'Hello, everyone—we'll see you as soon as we can,' and there was no disguising the lightening of the atmosphere and a general undercurrent of excitement as they recognised 'Dr Medic'. He might well be killed in the rush to see him, reflected Kerry with amusement.

'This is Dr Frank O'Mara's brother,' she explained to the room. 'As some of you may know, Dr Frank's had a bad accident and his brother, Dr Denovan, has kindly volunteered to help this morning. I take it most of you have seen him on the telly so I hardly need to introduce you to him!'

Freda was staring over the counter at them as they came into the office, her expression a picture of incredulity.

'You are him, aren't you—that Dr Medic?' were her first words to Denovan.

He grinned good-humouredly. 'I'm Denovan O'Mara,' he agreed. 'I'm just helping out a bit.'

Kerry stepped in hastily—she had an idea Freda would waste precious time questioning Denovan about life in the media and probably ask for his autograph for herself and her friends if she had the chance!

'It looks like chaos in the waiting room,' Kerry said. 'Are these patients all booked in?'

Freda rolled her eyes dramatically. 'I've no idea as none of the computers are working. I think last night had something to do with it. What patients shall I send through first?'

'The very young and the elderly should get priority—but if you see anyone obviously injured, send them first. If you're not sure, ask me.' Kerry flicked a look back at the waiting room and the strained faces of the patients. 'I wouldn't normally ever do this,' she declared, 'but these people look shocked. When Daphne appears can you give everyone a small cup of coffee? There's a pack of polystyrene cups in the cupboard. I think a bit of TLC is in order and they're going to have to wait for much longer than usual.'

She and Denovan went through to Frank's consulting room and Denovan sat down at the desk and whirled round in the chair with a grin.

'I never thought I'd be doing Frank's job,' he remarked. 'If he knew, he'd probably be furious—I'm the last person he'd want to be filling in for him.'

Kerry frowned. 'He ought to be grateful to you for helping. I know I am. I'm afraid you're going to be thrown in at the deep end, but if you need to ask anything you'll just have to knock on the door as the computers are down. I think it'll be a very haphazard list—some people won't have been able to make it over the bridge to see us, and we'll have others who've come at the last minute.'

Denovan nodded. 'I'll do my best,' he said as Kerry left. He pressed the button to activate the screen in the waiting room to call in the first patient. A burly middle-aged man limped very slowly and awkwardly into the room, his mouth a grim line of pain. Denovan indicated the chair on the other side of the desk.

'Do sit down,' he said.

The man shook his head and grimaced. 'If I do, I'll never get up, Doc. My back's gone—it feels really bad. I've done something to it and I can hardly move.'

He clung onto the back of the chair and Denovan looked at the man's face, noting his pallid complexion

and the slight sheen of perspiration on his forehead—
he was in great pain and it was obviously more than
a muscle strain.

'I think we've met before, haven't we?' Denovan
asked the man as he went round to examine his back.

The man nodded. 'I was with that lot helping last
night to get Sirie Patel free and then I helped to sta-
bilise the stretcher as we got her up to the surgery in
Dr Latimer's car. My name's Gerry Cummings.'

'Of course, that's it! You did a great job there,
Gerry—everyone did. We wouldn't have got Sirie
out before the river burst its banks unless we'd had a
team like yours.' Denovan rubbed his hands together to
warm them. 'Let me just feel the area,' he said, pulling
Gerry's shirt up. He ran his fingers lightly down the
spine and looked at the alignment of the man's back,
although it was hard to assess as poor Gerry was locked
in a stooped position.

'I'm going to give you some painkillers—quite
strong ones,' Denovan said, going back to his desk
and starting to write out a prescription. 'They'll also
help the muscles relax as they're in spasm at the moment and that's causing some of the pain. But more
importantly, when they get a helicopter down here I
want you to be taken off to have an X-ray as soon as
possible. You may have dislodged a disc when you were
heaving all that stone about.'

He handed Gerry the prescription and the man
looked worriedly back at him. 'Do you think it's serious? My wife's expecting and she's due any time now.
I'm supposed to look after our little girl while she has
the baby.'

Denovan shook his head. 'I'll be honest with you.

I don't think you'll be up to looking after a child at the moment. Can a neighbour help out? And another thing, if your wife's due to deliver a baby imminently I think she should be on the helicopter, too—just to be on the safe side!'

Gerry Cummings looked in dismay at Denovan. 'She won't fly,' he said dolefully. 'I don't think I'll get her on a helicopter for love or money!'

'Perhaps I can have a word with her?' suggested Denovan. 'And I'm going to find out the latest news on the helicopter and get you booked on. Do you have a mobile? Give me the number and I'll contact you.' He watched as Gerry started to inch his way painfully to the door. 'If you can get hold of a walking stick, that should help support you,' he suggested.

Gerry managed a wry chuckle. 'Perhaps I can borrow my father's Zimmer frame…'

The morning was filled with people like Gerry—many of them traumatised by what they'd gone through, worried out of their minds about the condition of their homes and the welfare of their children or elderly relatives. One couple, who had a shoe shop in the village, had battled all night to try and save their stock, to no avail, and the man had a deep gash on his arm where a metal box had fallen on him.

'I'm the third generation in the business—my grandfather and father built it up from nothing—and I can't bear the thought that this might be the finish of it,' said Peter Whittaker, looking mournfully at Denovan as the doctor swabbed his wound with disinfectant and held the skin together with steri-tabs.

'It's awful for you,' said Denovan sympathetically. 'I take it you're insured?'

Peter nodded. 'Oh, yes, we're insured for the loss of stock and putting in new fitments. But we're just starting our busy season when all the walkers come in for boots and trainers and that sort of thing. If the shop's not up and running we stand to lose a hell of a lot, and I dare say it will take months to sort things out.'

His wife, Donna, put a comforting hand on her husband's arm. 'We'll get my brothers to come and help us clean up. You'll be surprised how quickly we'll get it up and running again.'

They smiled at each other and Peter patted her hand. 'Of course, love—no good looking on the bleak side, is it?'

Denovan watched them go out rather wistfully. They were a lovely couple, obviously totally supportive of each other and not much older than him. They didn't lead a glamorous life and they probably worked a darned sight harder than the wealthy people he mingled with, but they were happy with each other and with their lives. He envied them.

He went over to the window and pulled aside the blinds. The room looked over the back of the medical centre towards the countryside and the patchwork of fields across to the hills. What would it be like to live in a place like this again? Very different from the sophisticated bustle and excitement of London, he guessed. But he had been brought up here and although his childhood had not been a happy one, a part of him longed for the open spaces and beauty of the countryside. He'd at least had freedom to run where he wanted and he'd been part of a small community that knew everyone, in contrast to the anonymity of a big city.

He turned away abruptly from the view and let the

blinds go with a snap. It was no good theorising about a life here—he didn't want to live or work anywhere near his half-brother anyway.

A tap at the door and Kerry came in. 'I think we're nearly through. How are you getting on?'

'I enjoyed it,' he said honestly. 'They've certainly all been through the mill, these people. There's one man who urgently needs an X-ray as he's injured his back badly, and I think his pregnant wife should be airlifted out as well.'

'I've been told a helicopter's on its way. I've treated an elderly man with a bad chest, and I'd be happier if he was out of here. We'd better contact these people and tell them to get to the field.'

Denovan looked at his watch. 'I'll go and relieve Daphne's sons from looking after Archie. I can't expect them to look after him all day. And then I'll go down and see how the bridge repair is going on.'

'I'll come down, too—I want to see the damage to the village, so I'll probably see you there when you've got Archie.'

In the cold light of day the damage to some of the houses looked catastrophic, and part of the road had become like a river, water swirling down the high street and onto the playing fields of the local school like a vast lake. In an odd way, it looked rather beautiful, with the sunlight making the water sparkle, and there was warmth in the air—it was hard to believe there'd been torrential rain a few hours before.

People were wading about in some of the houses, trying to salvage possessions, hauling them up the stairs to another storey, and in the homes higher up the hill, where the water had receded slightly, attempting to brush the water away.

In the little square a man with a microphone and wearing fisherman's waders, with a camera trained on him, was interviewing someone. Trust the media to get a camera into the place somehow, when no one else could get in or out! Kerry recognised the man being interviewed as the local MP. Tall, white-haired and imposing, Sir Vernon Hood was generally regarded as being good at his job, but there was an arrogance about him that revealed he was very aware of his position. Kerry reflected that she hadn't seen him for some time. At one time he'd been present at all the local functions, glad-handing everyone. Cynically she thought that he'd probably appeared just to show his concern over the disaster in Braxton now that it was headline news. She flicked a look at him as she turned away and the thought struck her that he looked much older than the last time she'd seen him—perhaps it was the shock of seeing what the flood had done to the place.

She went up to a woman she knew as a patient, who was leaning against her doorstep looking bleakly into her house. The woman shook her head in a despairing way. 'It's the smell and the mud...it's just horrible. We'll never get it right again.'

She dabbed at her eyes and Kerry hugged her. 'It will be OK eventually, Mary. They've got marvellous machines now that can dry places out and pumps that will get rid of this water. I believe the army's bringing equipment over the river to help everyone.'

Mary gave her a tremulous smile. 'At least we can have the place redecorated—we've been meaning to do it for months!' She jerked her head across at Sir Vernon Hood, still talking to the interviewer. 'I hope his nibs will do more than talk a lot of hot air like he usually does and get things moving! He promised us flood defences years ago but I haven't seen anything yet.'

Kerry made her way slowly back up the hill, wondering how long it would take to get things back to normal, and thinking wryly that it would be more difficult than ever to get a locum doctor to help out over the next few weeks.

'Things are pretty bad, aren't they?'

She looked up, startled out of her reverie, to see Denovan's tall figure standing in front of her. She nodded. 'Worse than I thought—the only good thing is that the sun's shining and it's stopped raining.' She looked at him, puzzled. 'Where's Archie? I thought you were collecting him?'

He smiled. 'Those boys of Daphne's are real gems. They've taken him to the field behind their house and are having a picnic. Archie's loving it. He doesn't get to do that kind of thing in London much.' He looked at his watch. 'I don't know about you, but I'm starving. I see that little café near the village hall is doing a brisk trade, but they might squeeze us in—what about a coffee and something to eat?'

There was hardly any room but they managed to squeeze into a corner of the shop, side by side, legs squashed together under a tiny table that would just about accommodate two people. She was aware that people were staring at them—or rather at Denovan! The whole village knew who she was and she could imagine their curiosity wondering why a celebrity doctor should be in their little village with her.

She flicked a look at Denovan's profile. No wonder

he'd got that job on TV. Up close she acknowledged that he was startlingly good-looking—firm lips, mesmerising blue eyes, the kind of eyes that when they looked into hers made her feel rather unsettled. And suddenly being quite so near him, feeling his muscular body next to hers, brought back the embarrassment Kerry had felt the night before. If she was any closer, she'd be sitting on his knee!

She took a deep breath and edged away slightly, trying to put some distance between them. Even if she was interested in Denovan O'Mara—which she definitely wasn't—she had to remember that this man was spoken for. The mother of his child had to be somewhere in the background of his life.

The light was dim in the café, the conversation around them a dull murmur, and Kerry leant back with her head against the wall and tried to put Denovan's disturbing proximity out of her mind. The young girl who came to serve them did a double-take when Denovan gave his order, pausing with her pencil hovering in the air before writing anything down.

'Oh, wow, you're that doctor person on TV aren't you?' She grinned cheekily at him. 'You look better than you do on that programme.'

'I'll take that as a compliment,' remarked Denovan wryly. 'Now, please would you bring us two coffees and two big plates of your best fish and chips?'

Kerry looked at him curiously when the girl had disappeared. 'Don't you find it a nuisance, everyone always recognising you?'

Denovan shrugged. 'You get used to it and I suppose it means that people are at least keen on watching the wretched programme.'

'*Wretched* programme?' enquired Kerry in surprise. 'Don't you enjoy what you do?'

He hesitated for a moment then said candidly, 'Perhaps not as much as I did. Of course London is a great place, but coming back here I can remember some of the good things about Braxton that I enjoyed as a little boy—the fresh air, fishing in the river and the beautiful surroundings.'

'You didn't want to be a GP here then, like your father and brother?'

He reached across the table and poured out two glasses of water, a guarded look on his face, but he said lightly, 'Better not to have too many O'Maras in one place.'

Kerry sighed. 'I imagine you have a glamorous life in London anyway, meeting lots of important people.'

Depends what you mean by glamorous, Denovan thought to himself. It was getting closer to make-your-mind-up day as far as his job in London was concerned as he had to let the powers that be know what he was going to do very soon. Did he like the job enough to go along with a new contract? Or if he decided to move on to pastures new, where would he go? He glanced at Kerry. She was the kind of colleague he'd like to work with, both reliable and feisty. Pity she was in the one place he could probably never live in again.

He grinned at her. 'I'm too busy to immerse myself too much in London's social whirl. Besides, the excitement begins to pall after a while.'

'And was Archie born there?'

'No. Archie was born in New Zealand. I came back to England a few months after his birth.'

Kerry flicked perceptive a look at him—she felt

there were many things unsaid behind those brief remarks. *Ah, well, everyone has a past,* she thought. *I'm not the only one with ghosts in the background,* but some devil inside her made her want to know more. She looked down at the table cloth and rearranged the cutlery slightly.

'And is Archie's mother in the media as well?'

'Archie's mother?'

Kerry looked up at him, startled by the harshness in his tone. 'I'm sorry. I don't want to pry.'

'Archie's mother is a free spirit,' Denovan said shortly. 'She joined some hippy community in Cornwall after we came back to England, and I don't think she thinks of Archie from one day to the next!' He took a deep gulp of water from his glass and an expression of deep sadness flitted across his face. 'Archie probably hardly remembers her at all.' And suddenly Kerry saw before her not the polished, glamorous, smooth celebrity, Denovan O'Mara, aka Dr Medic, but a father who loved his child very much and who suffered the same anxieties and worries as any man would, trying to protect that child from harm.

'I'm sorry,' she began inadequately.

'It wasn't Lorna's fault. She'd always made it clear that she never wanted a child.' His forlorn words hovered in the air, giving away a glimpse of his private life. 'I was the one to blame. I thought she would change her mind, but I was wrong.'

'You can't blame yourself surely?'

'Oh, but I do,' he said simply. 'One can't force people into being what they're not, and Lorna will never be maternal.' A wry grin twisted his mouth. 'And it could be I'm just too damn difficult to live with. It taught me one thing—commitment's a very serious step. Don't make it lightly! It'll be some time—if ever—before I contemplate settling down!'

Kerry nodded, but felt an odd flicker of disappointment. She wasn't surprised Denovan was wary of starting another relationship after his experience, but perhaps she'd been secretly hoping that he'd have changed his mind.

'And now...' He changed the subject abruptly. 'Enough about me. I believe you were all set to go on holiday until Frank messed it up?'

'How did you find that out?'

'I nearly fell over the suitcase in your bedroom when I brought your cocoa up last night.'

She shrugged. 'It's true. I should be lounging on a beach under a hot sun in Tobago today, preparing to be my cousin's bridesmaid on Friday.'

'That's too bad...perhaps another time?'

She laughed. 'I've no more cousins getting married!'

'You'll have to wait until it's your turn to get married, then.'

Kerry ignored the little knife that twisted in her chest. 'Maybe one day,' she said lightly.

'Come, now,' he said teasingly, giving her a penetrating look. 'I can't believe you don't have some adoring guy in the background.'

'No adoring guys, not even in the far distance.'

Then the waitress appeared with a huge tray of food, which she put on the table in front of them. 'Here you are, folks, fish and chips for two. Enjoy!'

Denovan grinned. 'Just what the doctor ordered. Let's tuck in.'

CHAPTER FOUR

'THERE'S a message from Laystone Hospital for Denovan to ring them,' said Daphne, when he and Kerry returned to the surgery after their lunch. 'At least the telephone lines have been repaired.'

While Denovan was ringing them back, Daphne gave Kerry a list of the home visits that had been requested that day.

'Looks like the army has done a great job with putting a temporary bridge up. I think you'll be able to get to most of these people now,' Daphne said. 'One of them is little Tilly Thompson up at Hill Farm— her chest is very bad. The call's just come in and her mother sounded very worried.'

'I'll go right away.' Kerry grabbed her bag and turned to Denovan, who had just finished his phone call. 'You'll be able to get back to London sooner than you thought. The road's open again.'

'Yes,' he said briskly. 'I should make it OK today, but I'll go and see Frank first. They've done a craniotomy to drain the bleed in his brain, and it seems he's holding his own. Then, of course, I'll get back as soon as possible as there's no point in hanging around here.'

'Of course not.' agreed Kerry, but there was something a little hollow about her agreement.

It wasn't only his help she would miss, Kerry admitted, but the man himself. She'd been prepared to dislike Denovan O'Mara, both from his manner when she'd first spoken to him about Frank and from what she'd heard about him from his half-brother. Funny how much her views had changed in twenty-four hours, she admitted. Denovan wasn't as bad as she'd thought he'd be. In fact, under the tough exterior there had been glimpses of a rather fun guy. And in the café just a few minutes ago she'd seen a loving father behind the glamorous celebrity image he projected. Even if she'd sworn lifelong celibacy, she couldn't help noticing that he was drop-dead gorgeous and exuded sex appeal!

She felt almost ashamed to confess even to herself that she'd felt the old thrill of attraction sitting next to a sexy-looking man, conscious of a vague feeling of disloyalty to Andy's memory. Then she bit her lip. She had to accept that Andy wasn't here now but Denovan was, and the fact that it was the first time she'd felt a frisson of magnetism for anyone since Andy had died showed that she was beginning to feel more human again. She told herself sternly that this was just a normal reaction to a good-looking man, because of course Denovan meant nothing at all to her. And she could mean nothing to him—he'd practically said that permanent relationships were not for him any more.

All the same, I don't want him to go, she thought, and then with a burst of honest introspection she acknowledged that it wasn't just because of his help at work but because she wanted to get to know more about Denovan O'Mara the man.

She said lightly, 'Give Frank our love. I imagine you're taking Archie with you to the hospital, then?'

'Don't worry about that,' interposed Daphne, who was sorting out prescriptions. 'You can't drag Archie to the hospital. The boys will be happy to look after him for another hour or two. I'll phone Larry on his mobile.'

'Those boys of yours are real stars,' said Denovan fervently. 'They deserve some decent remuneration. I'll pick Archie up on the way back from the hospital, but I'm so very grateful to them.' Denovan unleashed one of his sudden, sweet smiles, then turned to Kerry, holding out his hand. 'I'll be off when I've picked up Archie, so I'll probably not see you until I come back up to see Frank again.'

His clear blue gaze locked on to her face almost as if he was trying to memorise it.

'Keep well,' he said softly. 'I'll be in touch with you about Frank's progress.'

His mobile rang and Kerry went out to her car, leaving Denovan conducting an animated conversation with the person at the other end of the line. He followed Kerry with his eyes as he talked—she was such a bright, feisty woman, and knock-down gorgeous too. She'd never admit that she'd find it hard to cope and he admired her for that. He just wished he could get to know her better. He sighed and tried to concentrate on what the person at the other end of the line was saying.

That would probably be the last she'd see of the hotshot celebrity doctor for a long time, Kerry reflected ruefully as she crossed the car park and got into her car. Then she shrugged rather irritably, cross with herself for thinking so much about Denovan. Putting the car into gear, she set off for Hill Farm out in the countryside.

The Thompsons lived on an isolated farm on a hillside outside Laystone. Bathed in sunlight today, it was picture perfect—the stone farmhouse, its outline softened by ivy, sheep grazing in the patchwork of stone-walled fields, and the fresh green of the trees. Still, Kerry guessed it was a hard life for Laura Thompson, the mother of two young children.

Laura's face was tearstained as she answered the door to Kerry's knock, a round-eyed little boy clinging to her skirt.

'I'm so sorry to bring you all the way out here, Doctor,' she said in a choked voice. 'I'm just at my wit's end with Tilly…she sounds awful. I didn't know what to do for the best.'

'Don't worry, Laura, that's our job. If you're worried about your little girl, you did the right thing.'

How often Kerry had had to reassure parents that they weren't making a fuss when their children were ill! Although sometimes, she admitted, it was the other way round, with people ringing up for a visit when there was nothing wrong with them at all.

Laura led the way to the large kitchen, the little boy pattering along beside her, but even from down the corridor Kerry could hear the stertorous, gasping sound of a child fighting for breath.

'We brought her cot down here because it's warmer,' explained Laura. 'And I've got all the pans and kettles I can manage boiling as I remembered a steamy atmosphere is a good thing for bad chests.'

'Absolutely right,' agreed Kerry. 'Anything to try and open up her airways a bit.'

Tilly was sitting in the middle of her cot, a picture of misery, half crying, her plump little face red and blotched, every intake of breath an enormous effort, and it was obvious that she had a high temperature. Kerry's heart went out to the child.

'Hello, darling, you do look poorly, poor little thing—but we'll soon get you better. Mum, would you put her on your knee please, while I have a listen to her chest?'

Laura looked more composed, the relief of having a professional to assess her little daughter giving her more confidence. She lifted the child out of the cot and cuddled her as she sat down on a kitchen chair, rocking her backwards and forwards.

'It's all right, pet, just let Dr Latimer listen to your chest through this funny little tube.'

Kerry closed her eyes, concentrating on the sounds in Tilly's lungs she could hear through the earpieces of her stethoscope. She bit her lip. Tilly's heart was galloping, her chest full of wheezes and whistling noises. It was getting increasingly harder for the little girl to get air into her lungs and they needed to get her to hospital as quickly as possible.

She hooked the stethoscope round her neck. 'Where's your husband, Laura? Can he look after your little boy while we take Tilly to hospital in my car? It's all right,' she said quickly and reassuringly as Laura's face began to crumple again. 'What Tilly needs is some oxygen, possibly some nebulised adrenaline or cortisone—that should help her enormously. I don't want you to worry.' Kerry gave a short laugh. 'That's a silly thing to say, isn't it? You can't help worrying, but I assure you this croup is very common in young children with a viral condition and hospitals are well used to treating it.'

Laura gulped back her tears. 'I'll call Bill on his mobile. He's out in the field at the moment, mending a wall. He can be here in a minute to look after Ben.'

Kerry took out her own mobile and punched in the numbers for Laystone Hospital. 'Fast Track Admission Department, please. It's Dr Latimer here. I need a paediatrician and anaesthetist on standby for an eighteen-month-old girl in acute respiratory distress. I'm bringing her in now.'

She looked at Laura's stricken face as the terrified mother heard the words 'anaesthetist' and gripped her shoulder reassuringly. 'Don't be alarmed, it's just a sensible precaution to have everyone we might need available.'

'I know, I know,' said Laura miserably. 'I've got to pull myself together.'

'You're doing brilliantly. You look after the little one and I'll get us there.'

Thank goodness the roads were passable, thought Kerry as she navigated the twists and turns of the country road that led from Braxton to Laystone. She went carefully, not daring to risk an accident. Having a child sure was a roller-coaster of emotions, she thought wryly, and she had no doubt that she would have been just as overwrought as Laura if it had been her daughter she was taking to hospital.

Tilly had been safely installed with an oxygen tent over her cot and Laura had been assured by the paediatrician that the little girl would be very much better within the hour, but that they would keep her in for twenty-four hours to monitor her. Tilly had fallen into a restless sleep, but Laura refused to leave her child's side, and the nurse went to get her a cup of tea, offering to get one for Kerry, as well.

'No, thanks. While I'm here I think I'd better go and see how Dr O'Mara is. It's a good opportunity to do it while I can.'

Laura put her hand on Kerry's arm. 'Thank you,' she said in a choked voice. 'I don't know what I'd have done if you hadn't been there.'

'Glad to have been of help,' smiled Kerry. 'I'll be in touch with you tomorrow to see how things are. I'm sure Tilly will be back to her bouncing self very soon.'

A small glow of pleasure and satisfaction fluttered through Kerry as she made her way down the maze of corridors to the high-dependency unit, where Frank had been taken to be monitored. There was a lot of stress in her work, but sometimes when she felt she had made a difference to the outcome of a situation it all became worthwhile. Then her thoughts drifted back to the myriad things she had to do that afternoon…more visits, and then loads of paperwork, the results of blood tests and hospital reports to catch up on when she got back to the surgery. Normally she could have coped for a week or two, she supposed, but with the added complication of the flooding and the extra problems that had arisen because of that, there was more pressure than usual.

Then, as sometimes happened unexpectedly, her darling Andy's voice came back to her, calm, quiet but firm. *'You'll be all right, we can get through anything together.'* That's how he'd been whenever she'd been worried, or something had gone wrong—a quiet tower of strength. She stopped for a minute and took a deep breath to calm herself. He wouldn't have wanted her to go to pieces just because life was going to be hectic, he would have told her to plough on and get on with things regardless. She straightened her shoulders and pressed the bell by the door of the high-dependency unit to gain admittance.

'Dr O'Mara's doing very well,' the sister in charge of the unit told her reassuringly. 'Breathing well on his own. His brother, Dr Medic…I mean Dr O'Mara…is just with him at the moment.' She smiled rather archly. 'It was quite a surprise to realise who he was.'

Another female who'd fallen for Denovan's charm, thought Kerry with amusement. She hadn't realised that Denovan would still be at the hospital. Perhaps she wouldn't have come to see Frank today if she'd known. She hated saying goodbye twice, but she went through to the bay where Frank was lying with his eyes closed, hooked to various bits of monitoring equipment—tubes supplying salts and glucose to replace vital bodily fluids, machines measuring his blood-oxygen and blood-pressure levels. Kerry stood quietly for a moment, listening to the faint ticks of the machines and watching the blips dancing across the lines of the monitors. She didn't like to interrupt Denovan's time with his brother.

Denovan was looking down at Frank and from where Kerry stood, his unguarded expression seemed quite detached: he might have displayed more emotion for a patient he'd never met before than what he was showing to his brother, Kerry reflected wryly. With a little shiver of disbelief she felt it was almost as if he hated Frank. Just what had happened between the two men that made them so at odds with each other? She found it hard to understand Denovan's attitude because although she'd never been very close to Frank socially, he seemed a reasonable and competent colleague who worked hard and seemed popular with the patients—she got on with him well. What was there to hate about him?

'Hello, Denovan,' Kerry said softly. 'How are things?'

He looked across at her in surprise. 'I didn't know you were coming to the hospital!' he exclaimed, coming over to her.

'I had to bring a young patient in unexpectedly and while I had the chance I thought I'd just come and see how Frank was doing.'

'He seems to be holding his own after yesterday's craniotomy and, as you can see, he's breathing by himself.' Denovan sighed. 'Poor blighter. I wish…' His voice faded away and Kerry looked at him questioningly.

'What do you wish?'

He said bluntly, 'I wish I could feel more sympathy for him, I suppose.' He looked at Kerry's shocked face and smiled faintly. 'I'm afraid we've never got on—and for various reasons we became at daggers drawn.' He shrugged. 'I guess we're just too different in character. Incompatible.'

'You should make it up with him. Brothers shouldn't have disagreements surely?'

'Depends what they disagree about, doesn't it?' he replied tersely. There was a moment's awkward si-

lence then he flicked a look at his watch and with a
change of tone said, 'I'm glad I've seen you. I'd like
to talk to you about something. Let's go into the corridor for a minute.'

Kerry followed him out of the room and looked at
him enquiringly.

'I've been thinking about how you're going to manage over the next few weeks,' he said. 'Are you sure you
can't get some help? You can see that Frank's going to
be a long time recuperating.'

Kerry shrugged. 'It sounds so heartless to think of
my problems at the moment when Frank has the biggest problem, but the fact is there's a huge shortage
of locums around here. Anyway,' she said brusquely,
'it's no good worrying, I'll manage OK. I'll just have
to, won't I?'

She tilted her chin determinedly and her petite figure braced itself as if preparing for a rough ride in the
future.

Denovan grinned at her. 'You've got the resolve
to do anything, I'm sure, but there are only so many
hours in a day.' He paused, looking down at his feet,
jingling some change in his pockets, then said rather
awkwardly, 'I've been speaking to my agent today and
she seemed quite amenable about deferring the signing of my new contract. She says I don't have to make
my mind up immediately. If you want, I could stay on
for, say, two weeks and help you out over the worst.'

Kerry stared at him, open-mouthed. 'But...but I
thought you had to get back urgently for work?'

'I've told you—they are prepared to give me breathing space and I'm happy to take it. I could do with a
break myself.'

She smiled wryly. 'It wouldn't be much of a break, helping in the practice, would it?'

'Believe me, I'd look forward to being a bit hands-on and not just giving advice and opinions on theoretical case histories. Don't you know that a change is as good as a rest?' His blue eyes rested on hers. 'I think we've proved over the past twenty-four hours that we can work rather well together.'

She said diffidently, 'Are…are you sure about this? And what about Archie?'

'Where there's a will there's a way—there's always the nursery in the village. I could bribe them to take him for two weeks, I think.'

Kerry took a deep breath, a mixture of emotions churning up inside her. Did she want to work with someone who seemed so at odds with his brother, her colleague? Could it lead to complications when Frank came back to work?

Denovan regarded her closely and frowned. 'You have a problem with me working here?'

'You and your brother don't get on—he could be annoyed with me for accepting your help,' Kerry replied honestly.

'I'll be working with you, not him. I'm sure he'll be relieved that someone's filling in for him, whoever it is.'

'I suppose…'

'Look, if he objects, I'll go back to London.' Denovan grinned at her, his eyes twinkling. 'At the moment he's not going to know anyway as he's out for the count, isn't he?'

Kerry tried to look disapproving then laughed. 'Don't be so cruel! OK, you're right—I do need someone, and you're the only person who's offered so, yes, I'm grateful to you if you're sure you're able to spare me the time. To be honest, it's a load off my mind.'

She felt overwhelming relief that the short-term worry of sorting things out was going to be shared and if she was honest, wasn't there another emotion crackling away as well? A kind of suppressed excitement at working with Denovan!

'Then it suits both of us—I get to do something useful, and you get a little support.' He looked slightly embarrassed. 'There's only one slight drawback for you, though not for Archie and I, but can we stay with you for a night or two until the pub reopens or I find somewhere else?'

'Of course. Though you're probably not getting much sleep in that small bed.'

'I never find difficulty in falling asleep.' He grinned. 'Tell you what, I'll get a take-away and a bottle of wine for this evening to seal the arrangement!'

Denovan watched her walk away and smiled wryly. He'd only told a few little white lies regarding his agent. He'd had to use all his powers of persuasion to get her to agree that it would be good for him to defer signing a new contract with the TV company for a week or two. The fact was that over the last two days he'd realised how much Braxton Falls meant to him, even though his childhood had some bleak memories. Now he was up here he wanted to spend a little more time in the place, allow Archie to breathe the fresh air of the country—the little lad barely knew what a live cow looked like!

And then, of course, there was Kerry. He folded

his arms and stared unseeingly out of the window in the corridor. Had she been part of the pull to stay in Braxton too?

Over the years since Lorna had disappeared he'd been out with several women, many of them blind dates set up by friends dying to marry him off. Some of his dates had been good fun and attractive—and most of them had been very keen to prolong their friendship. Too keen. Many of them had been excited to be with someone who was in the public eye—he was never sure if they were more attracted by the thrill of going out with a so-called 'celebrity' than their liking of him, but there was no thrill of the chase, just coy allusions to happy married life and future plans. Most of the girls were pleasant with Archie, a few ignored or even resented his little son, but naturally they couldn't feel for him as he did as a father.

But Kerry, well, she was different. Feisty when she wanted to be, not too cloying with Archie—just natural. He could tell she'd be someone he'd like to work with. And there was something else, too—a flicker of that special attraction he'd found so elusive with other women. He didn't think she was the type to care whether he was well known or not. The truth was, she was gorgeous and he wanted to get to know her better, to know what made her tick. That certainly didn't mean that he wanted a permanent relationship, his young son came before any romantic commitment, but surely a brief encounter was allowed? Forty-eight hours seemed too soon to say goodbye!

A slight smile played over Denovan's lips. It was a paradox that two days ago he'd hated the thought of coming back to Braxton Falls and all the memories it held for him, but all of a sudden the picture had changed. The place was imbued with an exciting and interesting aura—and mostly due to Kerry Latimer!

The afternoon passed by in a haze for Kerry. A few hours ago she'd been worried out of her mind about how she would cope and now, even if it was only for a short time, she had some respite from the problem. And not just that, of all people it was Denovan O'Mara who would be working with her! She was feeling pleased because he was a good, competent doctor, she told herself sternly, and not because she felt this peculiar kind of excitement when he was near her. He wasn't even the type of man she went for—he wasn't quiet, diffident or unassuming, like Andy. He was full of macho confidence, probably opinionated and well aware of his own abilities and used to fawning adulation, as well! But the main thing was, she told herself, he would be a reliable colleague.

There wasn't much room in her little cottage for quiet reflection with an energetic little boy to be bathed and put to bed. Kerry was refreshing her make-up in her bedroom and could hear roars of laughter from the bathroom and then a lively game of tag being played up and down the stairs. Denovan and Archie had a great relationship.

She looked at her reflection in the mirror—thick glossy dark hair held back from her face by two combs, and wide hazel eyes that looked back at her with a sparkle of excitement in them. It was odd that she felt this animated about having a take-away and a bottle of wine. Of course it wasn't a date but, as Denovan had said, it was a sort of celebration, and she'd had so little to celebrate over the past year that that was excitement indeed.

It was cosy in the little sitting room with the curtains drawn, and there was even a small log fire burning in the grate, which Denovan had insisted on lighting. He looked far too big for the room, thought Kerry with amusement, his head almost brushing the ceiling, and when he sat down his long legs seemed to stretch right over the carpet. He handed her a glass of red wine.

'Cheers!' He grinned at her, sipped the wine and grimaced slightly. 'Not the best vintage, but it's the top of the range at the corner shop—where, by the way, I learned from Sirie's husband that she's doing really well and should be home fairly soon.'

'That's great. It seems ages since we had all that drama. Can you believe that it was only about forty-eight hours ago? So much has happened.'

'I know. And even after all the destruction, there's been an amazing community spirit here in Braxton. It's one of the attractions about the place, that and the beauty of the countryside.'

'Do you miss it?' asked Kerry, looking at his wistful expression.

He gave a short laugh and tossed back his wine in two gulps. 'It's been years since I lived here and, to tell the truth it wasn't the happiest of childhoods, but when I see the hills and the dales I realise that part of it will never leave me.' He smiled at her. 'I take it you intend to stay here?'

'I hope so—I love it.'

'Just happy times here, then?' He looked at her with a grin, refilling his glass after he'd emptied it so quickly.

Just happy times? To her horror Kerry felt the familiar prickle of tears well up in her eyes when she was reminded of what might have been, and a deep flush of embarrassment spread over her cheeks. She tried to smile, cover up the awkward pause, then swallowed hard. 'Not…not always, of course.'

The periwinkle-blue eyes missed nothing and he frowned. 'Hey,' he said softly, 'I've put my foot in it, haven't I? I'm so sorry. Did something happen?'

Kerry looked down at her hands and started to pleat, very precisely, the cream shirt she was wearing. 'It's nothing,' she mumbled. She didn't want to dwell on her past—she had to come to terms with it.

'Oh, come on, now,' he said gently, pulling back a tendril of hair from her forehead, his glance sweeping over her face, 'We're going to work together—I have to know some things about you. Tell me what went wrong.'

She would never have thought the tough, arrogant Dr O'Mara could be this sympathetic, this kindly, and why shouldn't she tell him the truth? It was common knowledge in the village that she'd been about to get married, and that suddenly it had all ended—the excitement of organising everything, the wonderful future they were going to have together—all gone in the space of a few seconds.

'There was someone,' she began haltingly, then ground to a halt, struggling to find the words to describe what had happened.

Denovan waited, watching her expression as she tried to compose herself. 'I get the picture,' he said gently. 'Something happened between you and someone you loved?'

Kerry gave a twisted little smile. 'You could say that. A year ago Andy Robinson and I were going to get married—Andy was a climber and also part of the mountain rescue team.' It was pointless going into the detail of the story, she thought, just deal with the facts. 'He was killed trying to help a couple who'd got into difficulties. It's hard to come to terms with.'

The words sounded completely inadequate, but their very simplicity added to the horror of the story, thought Denovan with a shiver of shock.

'I'm so very sorry,' he said softly, putting his hand over hers.

Kerry dashed the tears from her eyes and shook her head. 'I'm sorry, this is ridiculous.'

'Of course it's not. You must have been devastated.'

He put his arm round her shoulders and hugged her to him. It was just a kind gesture, she knew, something that anyone might do, but there was such comfort in it and strangely she felt soothed—even though Denovan was a man she hardly knew. Telling him about Andy seemed to have acted like balm on the open wound of grief. How odd that someone she had been wary of only a short time ago could help her in this way.

'Look,' he said softly. 'Ghastly things happen, things that you think you'll never get over—but life goes on, and somehow you learn to live with what happened.'

'That sounds as if it comes from the heart,' murmured Kerry, looking at his face and its fleetingly sad expression in the flickering firelight. 'I…I suppose you mean Archie's mother leaving you?' she questioned with hesitation.

He shook his head. 'No—I wasn't referring to that. To be honest, it was a relief when Lorna and I parted—

we were totally incompatible and things were pretty difficult between us. I was only desperately sad for Archie. It's very tough that he should never know his mother, because I know only too well from my own experience...' He stopped in mid-sentence, then said gently, 'But we weren't talking about me—you were telling me about Andy. I'm so, so sorry. You've had a lot to cope with, and now you've got to deal with all this bother of my brother having an accident.'

'Your brother was very kind when Andy died—easy to talk to.'

'I'm glad, but having to cope now on your own at work must be doubly difficult, especially with the floods.' His smile was kind and his finger went under her chin and gently turned her face towards his. 'Not many people could cope like you have.'

'I can deal with it. Please don't worry,' she said rather breathlessly.

She was aware that somehow the atmosphere between them had changed, become more personal, intimate. She was confused by her own conflicting emotions and the proximity of Denovan. Every nerve in her body was aware of how dangerously close she was to him. She was sure that something—she couldn't articulate just what it was—was about to happen and her heart bounded uncomfortably into overdrive.

'Seems we've learnt quite a bit about each other in the past twenty-four hours, haven't we?'

'Yes. I suppose so.'

'And one of the things I've learnt about you, Kerry, is that you're one feisty woman.'

His arm was still around her, holding her against him, and he leant forward and brushed her forehead with his lips. She didn't draw back. Rather she allowed herself to imagine the sweetness of his mouth on hers—because wasn't this secretly what she had been longing for, perhaps even needing? She closed her eyes, willing him to kiss her on her lips, for his arms to pull her towards him. After all these empty months of grieving for Andy it was as if every erogenous nerve in her body had been galvanised. She allowed herself to lean against this man she hardly knew and it felt natural and right and wonderful.

In the back of her mind a little voice whispered, *You're mad—you've only known this guy for two days!* Whatever Denovan said, they were still almost strangers. She didn't know his background or what sadness he referred to in his past, and he'd only brushed his lips across her forehead, but in that moment she'd realised that she had been attracted to him from the first moment she'd seen him. She pressed her lips to his cheek, responding to his feather-light kiss with eagerness, giving in to the clamour of her own longing. A kind of dizzy freedom from the sadness and constraints of the past year swept through her, and she couldn't help her response—an almost compulsive need to make love to this man she'd only known for a short time.

Then suddenly there was the sound of the wooden door being opened and banging against the wall behind them.

Denovan gently drew back from her and turned round to see who was there.

'Daddy…Daddy, I want a drink and I can't get to sleep.'

Archie's forlorn little figure stood in the doorway, clutching a teddy, illuminated by the light from the hallway. Denovan gave Kerry a half-shrug of apology before leaping up from the sofa and going towards his son, catching him up in his arms.

'Hello, sweetheart, of course you can have a drink. How about another story? You'll soon drop off then.'

'What were you and that lady doing?' asked Archie in his clear little voice.

Denovan laughed. 'Just getting to know each other,' he said lightly.

He took the little boy upstairs and Kerry watched him go with wistful thoughtfulness. What a fool she was if she believed that Andy's place could be taken by a man like Denovan—he had other things to think about, like his little boy. And, of course, Archie would always come first in his life. Any romantic interest would be put on the back burner because Denovan's priority would naturally be his child. And hadn't Denovan made it clear that he wasn't on the lookout for a partner?

Kerry stood up and touched her lips. Even in that brief contact against his cheek, they tingled with the memory. She shook her head in confusion—his friendly gesture of comfort had allowed her to think for a moment that she and Denovan had some kind of future, and how deluded and stupid was that? No good falling for a man who wasn't interested in romance before he went back to London and his glamorous life. If she didn't want another broken heart, she'd better keep well away from Dr Medic and regard him strictly as a colleague for the next two weeks.

CHAPTER FIVE

How quickly the two weeks had gone. Kerry had really been grateful to Denovan for his support because the surgery had been working at top capacity—one person would have found it impossible to cope. The floods had taken their toll on the villagers mentally and physically. It was surprising how many accidents had happened with people trying to salvage goods from houses ruined temporarily with flood water—putting their feet through rotten floorboards or cutting themselves on broken glass. Liz Ferris, Denovan or herself had spent nearly every afternoon patching people up with bandages or stitches.

And now, thank goodness, it was lunchtime on Friday and, whatever happened, Kerry was going to have a rest over the weekend, although she rather dreaded the next week when Denovan left Braxton.

She flicked a glance at him as she munched on a sandwich in the office. He was standing in front of the computer, his tall body half bent towards it as he ran through the hospital referral emails on the computer, his dark hair endearingly rumpled and a little too long over his collar. She reflected rather wistfully that there'd been no more intimate moments alone with

Denovan during these hectic two weeks, although she was intensely aware of his presence when he was in the room with her. But she'd been very firm with herself—no hint of flirtation with him, being businesslike and brisk at work and spending many an evening staying late at the surgery. She wasn't going to embarrass him again.

How stupid she'd been to come on so strongly to that casual comforting hug he'd given her two weeks ago—and how embarrassing it had been to see him the next morning at breakfast-time. He'd just been a ship passing in the night, and was only going to be with her for two short weeks. For heaven's sake, he must have thought she was completely sex-starved! And he wouldn't have been far from the truth, she thought wryly.

She recalled how Archie had been sitting in the little kitchen, eating some cereal, when she'd come down the morning after, and Denovan had been squeezed behind the table, drinking a cup of coffee.

'Would you like some of my great coffee?' he'd asked with a smile, holding up the coffee jug. His blue eyes had seemed to hold hers like a magnet. 'I hope you've recovered from the events of yesterday!'

Kerry hadn't been sure if he was making some coy allusion to what had happened between them the previous night, but she'd refused to react to it. It had meant nothing to him, and she was going to treat it the same way—however difficult it was. She'd ignored the last part of his sentence.

'It's OK, thanks. I'll just go straight across to the surgery if you don't mind,' she'd said lightly. 'There's some paperwork I must get down to, and I want to know what's happened to one of my elderly patients with an acute chest infection—he was taken by helicopter to hospital when the bridge collapsed. Daphne will give you a list of your patients when you've got Archie settled.'

She'd practically run out of the house, only pausing to grab a jacket from the row of hooks by the front door. She wouldn't give him any cause to be frightened of her!

They hadn't been alone much since then—Archie had had two little friends for a sleep over during that time, Denovan had been over several times to see his brother in hospital, now making good progress and in a general ward, and there had been two night home visits, which they'd taken in turns to do. Sometimes she'd seen Denovan looking at her rather intently and once he'd put a hand on her shoulder as he'd bent over to show her something on the computer and a thrill of excitement had zipped through her body as if she'd touched two electric terminals, but mostly she'd managed to keep her distance.

Kerry sighed and threw her half-eaten sandwich into the bin. Denovan would be gone next week so she could relax. She started to look idly through one of the many medical journals that arrived every day and Denovan stood up from the computer and stretched to relieve his back. His gaze flickered over to Kerry and unconsciously he clenched his fists in his pockets. She looked incredibly efficient and sexy in that neat white collared blouse with her thick hair in a neat pleat at the back of her head and a leather belt emphasising her small waist. Why the hell hadn't he made more of an effort to get to know her better, to be alone with her?

He was even staying in the same tiny cottage with her, for heaven's sake, and yet for some reason it had never seemed the right time to get closer.

With a certain grim humour he reflected that in London he wouldn't have had this trouble—women seemed almost too willing to encourage him. Perhaps the answer was, he told himself flatly, that Kerry Latimer wasn't at all interested in him. And yet two weeks ago he'd have sworn that she'd responded with more than a little eagerness to his brief kiss, although the next day she'd certainly been brusque enough with him at breakfast-time. When he'd offered her coffee, she'd refused and practically run out of the house.

'Was that a brush-off, Archie?' he'd murmured to his little son as he'd poured himself another cup of coffee. Perhaps she'd been trying to tell him something— possibly that he should step back a few paces and not assume that his affectionate gesture the night before had meant anything at all to her.

And yet just the briefest touch of her lips on his face had set an astonishing longing burning inside him. Lorna leaving him and their little son so abruptly had left him embittered. He had been very careful since then not to get involved too much with any woman, however attractive she was. Now he acknowledged, almost with surprise, that if Archie hadn't appeared at the very moment he'd kissed Kerry that night, he might have thrown caution to the winds.

And now two weeks had passed and it was as if they'd only just met, that brief kiss the only memory he had of something more intimate between them. He smiled grimly to himself. The truth was that he found Kerry the most irresistible and breathtaking woman he'd ever met, and his heart had melted when he'd seen her tears at the mention of her fiancé. Perhaps he'd been grossly insensitive, coming on to a woman whose heart had been broken by the death of her fiancé—a tragedy that she'd obviously not got over. How crass was that? He scowled unseeingly into space. Had he ruined any relationship he might have had with Kerry, even if it wasn't going to be lifelong commitment?

And yet…and yet he was sure that there had been something electric between them. He could swear that he hadn't been deluding himself when he'd thought she had responded to his kiss with something a little more than acquiescence. He closed his eyes for a moment and recalled the soft feel of her full lips on his mouth, the moulding of her body against his hard frame. How sweet it had been and how long ago since he had felt that magnetic attraction with any girl! But the way she'd rushed out of the house that morning had shown that she had been embarrassed by him—probably thought he'd taken advantage of her. Perhaps he ought to have apologised. What a waste of two weeks it had been! The only thing vaguely positive, he supposed wryly, was that he and Frank were at least communicating in a stilted way with each other.

'Daddy. Daddy! Here I am. We can go to the shops now. Daddy, you're not listening.'

Archie's indignant face swam into focus in front of Denovan and he started guiltily. He'd entirely forgotten that he was taking Archie in his lunch hour to buy some provisions for a picnic they were going on the next day.

'Oh, OK, Archie, I'm ready. We'll just go down to the corner shop and I'll drop you back for your last afternoon at the nursery.'

Freda and Daphne were gazing dolefully at the computer. 'The blasted thing's going round in circles,' Daphne informed Kerry. 'It keeps telling me I've made an illegal move. I've tried to ring the helpline but I can't get through. I guess it's something to do with the electrics and the flood.'

Kerry dumped her bag on the table in the office and sighed. 'Do we have any idea who's on the list?'

'Not really, we'll just have to take people as they come. Oh, and there's the baby clinic and I'm afraid Liz rang in to say she's got a stomach bug, so she can't do it.'

Kerry closed her eyes and groaned. Could anything else go wrong? 'That's all I need! Perhaps you could ask Denovan to do that clinic, then? He'll be in soon, he's just taken Archie to the shop in his lunch hour to get some picnic food.'

'We're going to miss him, that's for sure,' said Daphne. 'He's been such a great help for you.'

'And he's so cool,' sighed Freda. 'All my friends tried to make appointments to see him.'

'Not unless they were ill, I hope,' retorted Kerry tartly. 'No wonder we were so busy if all your friends were turning up in perfect health! Would you pass me those files, Freda, please?'

Freda handed her a sheaf of files and prattled on unconcernedly. 'Apparently Dr O'Mara's got so many women in London after him that he's hardly ever seen with the same woman twice!'

Kerry couldn't help laughing. 'I don't know where you get your information from.'

'Oh, he's in all my favourite celebrity magazines,' Freda informed her eagerly. 'Look, there's a gorgeous photo of him on the front cover of this one, and a great article inside about him and who he's been out with.' She thrust the magazine into Kerry's hands. 'Why don't you look at it when you've got a minute?'

Kerry's eyes met Daphne's amused expression. 'Honestly, Freda, you'd believe any old trash you're told about celebrities. Now, Daphne, would you ask the two-thirty patient to come in? We might as well start the ball rolling. I haven't time to pore over magazine articles!'

As she walked into her consulting room Kerry reflected wryly that Freda's gossip magazine was probably only too true—someone like Denovan in the public eye, invited to every media event in London, could have his pick of females and doubtless enjoyed every minute. What man wouldn't? She flicked an idle glance at the magazine cover. Freda was right, Denovan did look gorgeous and, despite her scorn of Freda's reading material, she knew she'd be looking at the article later on!

Kerry recognised Sir Vernon Hood MP as soon as he came through the door and recalled seeing him the day before being interviewed again by the media. Once more she thought how much he'd aged. He certainly didn't look his usual debonair self. He seemed thin, careworn, his eyes rather sunken and his usually upright figure stooped and frail. What had happened to the man? He was no longer the urbane figure who stood out in public meetings, appeared on television in Parliamentary debates, or opened fetes so charmingly.

He sank down into the chair opposite Kerry. 'How can I help you?' she asked pleasantly.

He leant forward, put his hands over his face and in a muffled voice muttered, 'I don't know...I don't know how to explain...'

There was something pathetic about this man and that was all the more extraordinary because he was a man who normally exuded confidence.

'I can try and help you,' Kerry said gently, 'if you tell me what's wrong.'

He looked up at her miserably. 'It...it's very personal...' he began.

'Look, that's what I'm here for. To try and sort out personal problems, physical or otherwise. You've managed to get yourself here, so you might as well tell me. There isn't much I haven't seen,' she said persuasively. 'Do you feel ill?'

Sir Vernon shook his head and said slowly, 'I'm a damn fool. I've jeopardised my life and my family's happiness. I've ruined everything.'

Kerry waited silently, giving the man a chance to talk. What seismic event had occurred to make the man look so defeated and diminished, almost haggard— such a far cry from the self-assured member of parliament striding through the village greeting people, perhaps, it had to be said, a little too much aware of his own importance and impressed by his own opinions? She knew that he had a glamorous, supportive wife and three young children who went to local schools. He seemed to have the perfect life.

At last he raised his head and began haltingly. 'I've

been in London for some time—I wasn't expecting to come back for a week or two. Then this flood occurred and of course I had to be here.'

Kerry nodded, not wanting to interrupt his flow. He looked beyond her, as if embarrassed to meet her eyes. 'The thing is, I should have been here when the waters started rising, before the river burst its banks and the bridge collapsed, but I didn't know that things were taking a turn for the worse.'

Kerry looked at him in surprise. 'You didn't?'

'No. I wasn't in the House of Commons, I was... er...busy elsewhere. My agent had tried to get hold of me but I'd lost my mobile so I wasn't getting any messages.'

'You didn't hear it on the news, or see it in the news-papers? We had journalists sniffing around for a few days before the flood. It's big news nowadays.'

For the first time his eyes met hers and after a sec-ond's pause he sighed and said in a flat voice, 'You might as well know the truth, I didn't know because, Dr Latimer, I was stoned out of my mind.'

There was a short silence and Kerry wondered for a second if she'd heard correctly. Sir Vernon Hood, respectable pillar of society, who served on numerous committees, a *druggie*?

He looked at her bleakly and shrugged. 'It's true, I'm a drug addict. When I should have been sitting in the House I was snorting cocaine in a hotel. I'm the lowest of the low.'

Kerry took a deep breath, trying not to let her inner astonishment show in her facial expression.

'How did you get into your addiction?'

A bitter laugh. 'The old story. I fell for a young

pretty woman who flattered me. London can be boring on your own at night, Dr Latimer. Somehow, through her I got inveigled into trying the damn stuff. I was very tired and the drugs seemed to perk me up—that and the odd glass of wine. It didn't take long to get a hold but now she's blackmailing me.'

There was a certain self-pity in his voice, and Kerry's sympathy dissipated. Why should she feel sorry for this man born to privilege with every advantage in life? He'd betrayed his wife and family just because he'd been bored in London and had needed a little excitement. No wonder he'd not been in evidence lately. He'd been having a sordid affair, and now that his comfortable life looked as if it might implode, he was terrified of the consequences.

He looked at her narrowly, as if guessing her true thoughts. 'You want to know why I've come to you, I suppose.' He leant forward, looking at her pleadingly. 'You've got to help me get free of these drugs. If Claudia spills the beans, the press will be down on me like a ton of bricks. At least if I'm clean I can say I've conquered the problem. I want to feel as if I'm in control of my life again.'

'It won't be easy. You've got to have a real resolve and help and support from those around you. Motivation is the key thing. Does your wife know about this?'

'I…I told her last night. I had to, because I'm frightened that if the hacks did get hold of the story they'd come to the house, and I wouldn't be able to keep it under wraps.' For the first time he looked ashamed. 'She'a a good woman. She's said she'll stand by me— whatever happens.'

'You're lucky to have that support.'

He grimaced. 'I guess I could be the next big story now—splashed across every tabloid in Britain. "MP in cocaine ring". That would be my career done for.' His voice faded away, then he looked at Kerry almost defiantly. 'So, what can you do for me?'

'I can refer you to the drug centre in Laystone, which will use a combination of medication and counselling to help your recovery.'

'Why can't you do it? You're my GP. I don't want to go anywhere else—anywhere I might be recognised. Good God, if I'm seen going into a drug centre, the whole world's going to know.'

'We don't provide those sorts of facilities here Sir Vernon. The centre is a place dedicated to the rehabilitation of drug addicts and we've found that because they specialise in the problem and devote all their time to it, there's more chance of success.'

'So you're not going to give me any treatment?'

'I can't—not at the surgery—only at Laystone. It's part of the hospital in a new wing...'

'I know where it is all right. I opened the place not five years ago! I didn't realise that it had completely taken over the GPs' responsibility for treating drug addiction.'

'Do you want me to refer you? It really would be a good idea after you've made the first move by coming for help. That's very commendable. You will have dark days with withdrawal symptoms, but the centre will give you treatment for that.'

The MP sighed. 'Then you'd better refer me. I'll have to hope people will think I'm going on some government business if they see me.'

Kerry printed out a referral letter and handed it to

him. 'I wish you luck, Sir Vernon. I'm sure you can break your addiction with their help. You've made a brave start by admitting you need to change your life-style.'

He nodded and went out slowly. It was tragic that the man had almost ruined his life and that of his family. What a fall from grace! The flood had had an impact on people's lives in many different ways—if Vernon Hood hadn't had to come back so quickly to Braxton Falls, he might have been able to wriggle out of his dif-ficulty somehow in London before the affair became public knowledge. But she suspected that he would have been found out sooner or later and the dignified front he presented to the public would have crumbled.

After the surprising revelations from Sir Vernon, the afternoon became busier and busier. Never had Kerry welcomed the end of the day with as much enthusi-asm as this. Although the computers were once more up and running, the results of the floods had thrown up a multitude of problems—she had a long meeting with the public health department over the worries of sewage from overflowing drains, and with Social Ser-vices about moving elderly and infirm patients out of houses that were no longer habitable. So much had to be squeezed into a short time and her brain felt so full of decisions to be made it was jumbled up like the in-gredients in a food mixer.

With a sigh of relief she said goodbye to her final patient of the day and stood up to stretch her stiff back, then picked up her handbag. The magazine Freda had lent her had been pushed into it, and she pulled it out. Denovan's photo stared back at her from the cover—blue eyes gazed gravely towards the camera, set in a clean-cut face, dark hair slightly tousled over his brow. A slight smile played on his lips, preventing him from looking too severe, but he didn't look too cheesy. Every girl's dream man, she thought wryly.

She flicked through the pages to the article about him—she might deem the mag a load of rubbish, but she certainly was going to read it! A montage of photos spread across the centrefold page showed Denovan in a variety of settings: in front of camera during a programme, with his arm slung round various glamorous-looking women at nightclubs, concerts and even film premiers. The largest picture had him looking into the eyes of a statuesque blonde who was leaning towards him in a provocative pose, glossy hair tumbling over her shoulders and a low-cut dress showing plenty of cleavage. In all of them he looked assured and perfectly at home in the sophisticated world he lived in.

'Hot Spot of the Week,' proclaimed the headline. *'Our hottest guy this week is dishy TV doctor Denovan O'Mara, who has everyone guessing who his latest love is! He remains cagey, saying that marriage isn't for him—we guess he's having too good a time, but rumour has it that his taste is for someone in the showbiz world called Suzy de Forno, featured in our main photograph. But when he's out of the public eye, the hot doc's priority is his little boy, Archie. Separated from Archie's mum, we say Denovan O'Mara's the most eligible bachelor in town!'*

Kerry threw the magazine irritably into a drawer. Even if she had been having a pleasurable fantasy about a liaison with Denovan, he was out of her league altogether. There were far too many reasons not to fall for the man! How could she hope to compete with someone like Suzy de Forno? Perhaps Frank's assessment of his brother as a womaniser had been right.

She went to the window and stared moodily at the little village below. Gloomily she supposed she was one of thousands of women who'd shown a marked interest in Denovan O'Mara—one only had to look at the photos in the magazine!

He was a man who had another life she knew nothing about—as Freda had said, a life filled with adulation, not only from viewers but from the women in his social circle. He wasn't likely to be excited by a woman in a little country place like Braxton Falls who had leapt on him at the least encouragement.

She had to get out into the fresh air, Kerry decided firmly, clear her head and have a good walk, away from the stuffy atmosphere of the surgery. She would have a brisk stroll when she'd dumped her things in the house and changed her clothes, and perhaps the change of scenery would put the darned man out of her mind. With a sigh of relief she turned off the computer, shoved some papers into a drawer and said goodbye to everyone in the office.

Kerry took a deep breath of the brisk, cool, evening air as she set out along the side of the hill beyond her house. The patchwork of fields below her still had large lakes of flood water spread over them, giving a different look to the countryside she was used to, but the evenings were getting lighter now, and the sky was a rosy pink over the hills against a pale blue sky. How could she live anywhere else? She pitied anyone who didn't have this countryside to refresh themselves in, these wonderful walks up and down the little hills and valleys. Gradually the stresses of the day seemed to fade and even the thought of Denovan returning to London was something she would get used to, she supposed. It was ridiculous to fall for the first gorgeous guy she'd met since Andy had died. Denovan wasn't available, full stop! And anyway, hadn't he said that although he loved it in Braxton, he could never live here because of the past?

Her stride lengthened as she reached the little copse that grew above the village, the leaves of the oaks and ashes beginning to uncurl and the hedges showing a haze of green as spring began to take a magical hold on the countryside. She began to think of the things she would do in the summer—play more tennis and go riding. There were stables in the next village, and there was nothing more exhilarating than cantering along the hillside on a fine evening.

Vaguely she heard footsteps some way behind her, then they came closer and she turned round, and with a jolt of surprise saw Denovan running along the path and behind him Archie's little figure was scampering as fast as he could to keep up with his father. Damn, she thought irritably, just when I thought I'd got Denovan O'Mara out of my head!

He drew up beside her, and she tried not to stare at his tall, rangy figure dressed in faded khaki shorts. Why did he have to be so attractive? The trouble was, men with his looks were thin on the ground in Braxton Falls.

'My goodness, you're a fast walker!' observed Denovan, his eyes sweeping over her slight figure. 'We saw you setting off as I brought Archie back from nursery and I thought that some exercise on an evening like this would be a great idea.'

'Please don't let me stop you, then,' Kerry said politely, the hairs on the back of her neck prickling under his scrutiny. 'I'm just having a quick stroll myself.'

Denovan grinned. 'We've run enough, haven't we, Archie? We'll just walk along with you, if that's OK.'

Kerry wanted to say that, no, it wasn't OK, that she'd come out to free her mind from work and concerns about him and not to find herself an inch away from the man and his splendid physique.

'If you want to, of course.' She looked down at Archie. 'And how was your last day at nursery, Archie? Did they have a good party for you?'

The little boy frowned. 'It was good, but I sat next to a girl who took my colouring pencils. I didn't like her.' He kicked a stone on the path. 'Luca's my friend—he's in London. I want to see him.'

Denovan's patted Archie on his head. 'You'll be seeing him next week when we go back.'

'Why can't he come here? It's good here. Larry's getting a puppy and he said I could play with it!'

'We can't stay here for ever. We've got to get back to the flat.'

Archie's earnest round face looked up at his father. 'Could we have a puppy in London?' Archie watched Denovan's negative expression and suddenly beamed at his father. 'I've got a great idea—we could buy a house here and I could have Luca to stay and get a puppy and a kitten and some chickens!'

'And what about my job, young man? How am I going to earn money to keep all these animals?'

Archie looked puzzled, then his face cleared. 'Kerry

has a job' He turned his little face up to Kerry, his round glasses making him look grave. 'You'd help him, wouldn't you?'

Kerry gave an embarrassed laugh. 'Your daddy already has a job on television—he can't be in two places at once! Besides, what about all the exciting things you do in London? Like playing in the park with your friends?'

Archie pursed his lips as if considering the idea. 'I do like the park…' His attention was suddenly taken by two rabbits chasing each other along the path. He gave a whoop of delight, and ran after them. 'Come back, rabbits…come back here!'

Denovan watched the little boy's flying figure proudly. 'He's certainly smitten with Braxton. This weekend I'm going to take him to a few of my childhood haunts—there's a little cave up in the hills with a waterfall that I used to love, and of course the miniature railway has opened up again at Laystone. He'll find that great fun.' He looked at Kerry. 'I don't suppose you'd fancy coming with us?'

'You're very kind but I'm afraid I haven't really time,' said Kerry quickly. 'I've got a tremendous amount to do…so if you don't mind…'

Was he being kind to her, including her in their activities because he assumed she didn't do much at the weekends? Or, thought Kerry cynically, pitching a line to her like the lothario he seemed to be, according to the magazine? Perhaps that wasn't fair to him, but she wasn't going to be drawn into his life any more than she had to be. She'd had a shock two weeks ago when she'd realised just how much she was attracted to Denovan, and the more she saw of him, the more attractive he seemed. She wasn't going to make a fool of herself again with a doctor who seemed to be the toast of London!

She flicked a glance at him—the casual outfit he was wearing definitely emphasised his athletic physique. She looked away again quickly.

'Oh, come on—it will only be for the afternoon and that gives you loads of time to catch up on things surely? Don't you think you deserve a bit of time off after the two weeks you've had?' He smiled at her persuasively, putting his hands on her shoulders, turning her to face him. 'I know Archie would love you to come and so would I, of course. After all, it is our last weekend here,' he added as a sort of casual afterthought, his blue eyes looking down at her compellingly.

Kerry hesitated, a feeling like an electric shock whipping through her body at the touch of his hands, and tried to avoid his eyes. If only he wouldn't come so close to her. It made every sensible thought fly out of her head. She drew back from that magnetic aura that seemed to surround him and pulled a leaf from a hedge, rubbing it nervously between her fingers.

'I'm not sure.'

Denovan gave her a shrewd look and spread his hands out, almost in supplication. 'Look, I'm sorry. Perhaps I got off on the wrong foot two weeks ago when I hugged you. I suppose I just wanted you to know how sorry I was for your loss—it won't happen again.'

Kerry looked at him in surprise, then forced a smile. 'Oh, that?' she said loftily, raising an eyebrow with a pretty good imitation of casual indifference. 'Don't worry, I knew you were just being very kind and understanding as you could see I was upset about Andrew. Of course I never assumed that you meant anything by it.'

Denovan thought wryly that he supposed it was a relief that his brief kiss had meant nothing to her at all, except as a gesture of kindness. He must have imagined Kerry's spark of response, the way he'd thought she'd pressed her soft body against him, and then her brush-off at breakfast-time. And what a fool he'd be to start a relationship anyway. He'd learned his lesson—too often he'd been duped by women in his life. Bitter experience had left him with little faith in women and love. And yet there was something about Kerry that he trusted, something about her that made him want to be in her company. Surely he could do that and not be compromised? 'Well, then,' he said jovially, pushing negative thoughts to the back of his mind, 'there's no reason for you not to come with us, is there, just for an afternoon of fun and exploration?'

How easy it had been to lie to him, reflected Kerry. He obviously hadn't noticed her over-eager response that night to his kiss! But now Denovan had made it clear that he had only been trying to comfort her and she was unlikely to be thrown into any intimate sort of situation with him, it was hard to refuse. It was just going to be a pleasant afternoon, a kind of farewell after the two weeks he'd worked at Braxton. Denovan was right, it had been a gruelling, tense fortnight and a little outing would be invigorating.

'OK, then,' she said brightly. 'Just for the afternoon, of course. It would be lovely.'

A boyish grin lit up Denovan's face, his eyes crinkling. 'Terrific! I know we'll have a good time. Don't forget to wear your walking boots tomorrow,' he added.

'It's quite a long way from the little railway to the waterfall—I shall be taking some drinks to help us on our way!'

'And I'll bring some snack food for a little picnic, as well. I know what Archie likes—biscuits and crisps.'

Denovan laughed. 'Yes, you can't go wrong with salt, fat and sugar with Archie.'

And even though she knew that Denovan was off-limits where romance was concerned, Kerry felt a thrill of excitement at spending an afternoon with him and his little boy. Suddenly the weekend had a purpose, and the promise of companionship and fun.

CHAPTER SIX

'DADDY, this is great! Can I get on that train now? I want to go in the front near the driver, I want to see him drive the train, I want...'

Archie bounced up and down in front of Denovan and Kerry, his cheeks pink, and eyes sparkling with excitement behind their owlish glasses. It was just the day for an outing, thought Kerry—warm sun, jolly crowds, and the pleasure of taking out a little boy to enjoy himself in a country theme park.

'OK, Archie,' said Denovan, laughing at the little boy's elation. 'Give the train a chance to stop at the platform.' He looked round at the little mock station and nodded in a satisfied way. 'This is just how it was when I was young,' he remarked. 'Actually, it's better than it was then, because I think they've made more of the scenery. They used to have a part that went through a wild wood with animated tigers and lions in it. I wonder if they've still got that?'

Kerry flicked an amused glance at him. He was nearly as excited as his son!

'Brings back happy memories, does it?' she asked.

'My mother used to bring me here when I was little—I thought it was heaven!'

The briefest shadow crossed his face, then he put a hand out to prevent Archie from running towards the miniature train as it came to a halt and disgorged its small passengers with their parents. It had several open carriages, and the little boy grabbed Denovan's and Kerry's hands.

'Come on,' he urged, pulling them with him. 'Let's get in now at the front.'

The driver turned round and smiled at them. 'Does the young man want to sit with me?' he asked. 'It's first come, first served, and it means he can ring the bell. Mum and Dad will have to sit behind us, I'm afraid, as there's only room for one beside me!'

Denovan eyes twinkled at Kerry. 'There you are, Mum! That's your role for the day.'

'I'll try and keep you both in order, then.' She smiled, a faint blush of embarrassment on her cheeks.

A look of bliss suffused Archie's face as he scrambled up beside the driver, and sat proudly very upright, holding on to the bell until told to pull it. He turned round and beamed at his father, informing him, 'I'm going to start it off!'

'That's made his day.' Denovan grinned. He turned to Kerry. 'Come on, you'll have to get in beside me. I can't wait to go down memory lane!'

Kerry squashed in, jammed tight against Denovan's muscular thighs. The small carriage hadn't really been constructed with men the size of Denovan in mind. She pushed herself into a corner as much as she could, pulling her legs to one side and trying to relax against the rather uncomfortable wooden slats of the seat, determined to try and keep her distance. Denovan had made it clear that this was to be a social outing, an afternoon for fun and entertaining Archie, and if she was too near the man she was sure her thoughts wouldn't just be about Archie!

The afternoon was turning out to be great fun, she acknowledged. The sun was shining, everyone looked happy—the flooding down the valley and all the devastation temporarily forgotten. She couldn't remember the last time she'd had the pleasure of going out and doing something different at the weekend. She gave a happy little wave to Archie as he turned round to look at them both.

Denovan looked covertly at Kerry's profile, with its tip-tilted nose and her cloud of dark glossy hair held back by two combs at the side, a blush of excitement on her cheeks. She looked so natural, so gorgeous! It was just as well that Archie was with them—if he'd been alone with her he didn't know if he could have kept his resolution to retain their relationship on a strictly friendly basis! He was intensely aware of her nearness, the fresh smell of her light perfume tantalising him, stirring far too many feelings that had lain dormant for a long, long time.

He flicked a look at the little crowd of people getting on the train with them—did they see a happy family unit of three, as the driver had? A daddy and a mummy and a happy little boy?

A forlorn sense of what might have been in his life suddenly surged through him. If only Lorna and he had made a go of it and she had taken to motherhood, Archie would indeed have been part of a family unit, instead of having to make do with a father who generally didn't have enough time to take him on outings, or various childminders who were kind to him but were merely doing a professional job. A rerun, he thought sadly, of his own life.

The bell clanged suddenly and Archie shouted excitedly, 'We're going! Off we go!'

Kerry turned to Denovan and laughed, her cheeks dimpling. 'I feel as if I'm going on a real adventure.'

And he laughed back at her, both of them caught up in the happiness of a little boy. Denovan put his arm casually round the back of the cramped seat and tried to stretch his legs, shifting in his seat and coincidentally getting even closer to Kerry.

'It seems much smaller in this carriage than it did when I was five,' he observed. 'Ah, we're coming to a tunnel now. I remember this.' He grinned, pointing to the arch. 'But I don't remember that notice over the top of it—"The Tunnel of Love to the Land of Enchantment".'

The little train gave a shrill blast of its whistle as it drew into the tunnel, and Archie shouted in the darkness. 'I pulled that whistle! I pulled that whistle!'

Then the driver's voice came over a loudspeaker. 'Gentlemen, as you saw, this is the tunnel of love—it's imperative to show the girl of your dreams how much you admire her!'

Kerry giggled rather nervously. It was all rather intimate and in the gloom of the tunnel she felt even more aware of just how close Denovan was to her. His arm was only touching her back lightly, but she was very conscious of that slight contact, and a treacherous frisson of attraction flickered through her body like a pulsating wave. She knew that he had turned his head towards her, she could feel his warm breath on her cheek, smell the faintly astringent scent of his aftershave. If only, she thought wistfully, he was just an ordinary guy and someone not in the public eye, who didn't appear to have a string of girlfriends—then perhaps she would have shifted slightly nearer to him, given him a little encouragement. But she was darned if she was going to join the throng of women who were apparently drooling over him in London.

Just how long was this tunnel? Every second in that suddenly private little world seemed to heighten the atmosphere between them, but perhaps Denovan didn't feel it, and it was only her fevered imagination that allowed her to imagine his lips on hers and his arms around her?

He gave a low chuckle and murmured, 'These are the most uncomfortable seats I've sat in for a long time.'

'Yes, aren't they?' agreed Kerry rather breathlessly.

Then suddenly they were in the daylight once more and Kerry blinked in the bright sun and Denovan put on dark sunglasses so that she couldn't see his blue eyes. When the train drew into the little station at the end of the ride, there was a crowd of children waiting to get on, and as Archie scrambled down from the driver's cab, he gave a shout of delight.

'There's Larry and the other boys and Daphne. Hi! I've been helping to drive this train. I blew the whistle! Can I go on again with them, Daddy?'

'We're going to the waterfall now, Archie. It's quite far away so we've got to get going before it gets cold.'

Archie's bright little face dropped. 'I want to stay here with the boys,' he muttered. 'I don't want to go to the waterfall today.'

'Let him stay with us,' suggested Larry. 'We'll look after him, won't we, Mum?'

'I can't let you do that,' protested Denovan. 'You've been looking after him for the past few days. Enough's enough!'

Daphne laughed. 'For goodness' sake, Denovan, we love having Archie and he seems to have a civilising effect on my lads. We actually came over to ask him to come with us anyway, but you'd gone out when we called round.'

Kerry bit her lip—the afternoon wasn't going quite as she'd planned. It was meant to be an outing for Archie now suddenly the stage seemed to be set for just her and Denovan to spend the next two hours totally alone.

'But we ought to stay here with Archie. After all, he doesn't see much of you during the week and we're having such fun,' she remarked hopefully.

'*I* don't mind,' said Archie brightly, adding reassuringly, 'Daphne will look after me!'

Daphne laughed and looked at the two doctors' faces. 'This is the first time in days I've seen you two looking at all rested and relaxed with some colour in your cheeks. The past two weeks have been a nightmare for you. You go and have an hour or two to yourselves. A good walk would do you good. Really, I insist!'

Archie looked pleadingly at Denovan. 'Go on, Daddy—let me stay with them!'

Denovan shook his head helplessly. 'Well, if you're absolutely sure…' He took out his wallet. 'But this I insist. I want you all to have a huge cream tea at the café here when you've done all the rides and slides you want. I'll see you back at the village. Can you fit him in your car?'

Archie gave a whoop of delight and hugged his father round his knees. 'Thank you, thank you, Daddy,' he shouted.

'It's Daphne and her boys you ought to be thanking, not me.' He turned to Kerry. 'Right you are, then. We'll set off for the waterfall—it should only take us about forty minutes from here if we walk briskly.'

One thing was clear, reflected Kerry, breathing hard as she tackled the steep hill up to the waterfall, she had to get fitter! It was embarrassing to trail behind Denovan as he strode briskly out across the path through the fields that bordered the adventure park. Of course, she hadn't done any proper exercise for a long time and it was showing in her feeble attempts to keep up with him. When Andy had been alive they'd delighted in going on long hikes over the moors, and without him she'd definitely been using the car too much, because somehow walking by herself had led to too much introspection and loneliness.

'I hope I'm not tiring you out,' remarked Denovan, his amused eyes watching her as she scrambled up towards him, her cheeks pink with exertion. 'At least it's getting your cardiac rate up.'

'Don't be ridiculous. I'm not a bit tired,' she retorted, taking a deep breath and trying not to gasp too much. It had become very humid, and surreptitiously she wiped her forehead with a hanky and ran a tongue over her dry lips. She pulled out her water bottle from her pocket and took a grateful swig. 'Just keeping myself hydrated,' she said defiantly. 'I'm in great shape, actually.'

'You certainly are.' he murmured, then bit his lip. Why was he flirting with her? Hadn't he decided that flirtation wasn't on the agenda?

Kerry looked at him sharply and decided to change the subject. 'So where is this waterfall? I think I can hear it.'

'Just round this corner—and then perhaps we can have a pit stop for some food.'

'Not on my account,' Kerry said loftily. 'I can certainly go on for ages yet.'

Denovan grinned sardonically. 'I'm sure you can. However, it's a good place to sit as there's a lovely view, and it will give us fuel for the next little trek.'

They turned the corner, and suddenly there was the waterfall, tumbling over a high rock in the hill, a never-ending torrent of water, sparkling silver in the sunlight as it plunged down into the river below in a cascade of boiling white foam.

Kerry stopped short and gazed up at it, mesmerised. 'Wow!' she gasped. 'And I never even knew this was where the falls were.'

'How long have you worked in the area, then?' Denovan asked. 'This is where Braxton Falls gets its name from, of course.'

'Goodness—quite a few years, but although I used to walk with Andy at the weekends, we'd go further afield because he was a warden in his spare time in another part of the Peak National Park. We didn't make it up here.'

'And he was a member of the mountain rescue team? A busy guy, I reckon. You must miss him very much.'

Kerry paused for a minute without replying, and frowned, trying to put her feelings into words. She realised with surprise that Andy's loss wasn't tearing at her heartstrings as much as it had even a few days ago, and she seemed to be able to talk about him without her eyes filling with tears any more.

'Of course I miss him. But I have to admit I think of him now with more happiness at the memory than sadness at the loss. Perhaps time is helping to heal things a bit.'

And there was something else that helped, Kerry reflected, trying to be honest with herself—she'd learned she wasn't immune any more to an attractive man. It was Denovan who was helping to heal the scars of living life without grief for Andy's death overshadowing it. Two weeks ago she'd still been in mourning for Andy but suddenly she was looking forward and not back to the past. Was it because a drop-dead gorgeous male had come into her orbit, even if he was off-limits? She flicked a glance at Denovan sitting near her on the grass, all too aware that they were alone together in this beautiful place with nothing to distract them but each other.

Denovan sighed and took off his rucksack, slinging it to the ground before he sat down. If only he could let go of the past, like Kerry had. Returning to Braxton Falls had brought too many painful memories back: he loved the place, but he had so many unresolved issues with his half-brother still weighing him down that it would be difficult to make a new life here. He smiled wryly to himself as he pulled a small bottle of wine from the rucksack. When he'd come up to Derbyshire three days ago the thought of moving back here had never entered his head, but now it didn't seem all that preposterous. Perhaps one day it might happen.

He shrugged and opened the wine, pouring measures into two plastic cups and handing Kerry one of them.

'Cheers! I think we deserve to relax after such a gruelling time over the last weeks.'

She raised a cup in his direction. 'And thank you for staying to help me out. I don't know how I would have coped if you hadn't been here. You were a star!'

His eyes locked with hers for an instant. 'I assure you it was a real pleasure.'

Kerry sat down rather self-consciously near him— but not too near. She took a gulp of wine and looked around, trying to concentrate on something other than Denovan and his disturbing presence. It was so lovely—the background sound of the waterfall, the warmth of the sun on her face, and high above a buzzard wheeling around lazily as it quartered the sky looking for prey.

Denovan's rangy body lay half-upright, long legs stretched out before him, his strong profile and tousled hair in relief against the green of the trees. He sipped his wine and smiled across at her. Perfect setting and a perfect man, Kerry reflected. So much for concentrating on something else and pushing him out of her mind.

'Penny for them. What are you thinking about?' he murmured.

'Oh, nothing really. Just thinking how lovely it is here. I feel as if I've come on holiday.'

'It's not quite Tobago, I'm afraid—I guess the wedding's taken place by now?'

'That's right. I spoke to Rachel just before the ceremony. She was very excited.'

It seemed a lifetime ago that she'd been packing excitedly to go to her cousin's wedding—and to her surprise she didn't have any pangs at all about not being there. She looked again at the tumbling, sparkling cascade of water.

'Actually, I think this is probably more beautiful than anywhere abroad,' she mused.

Denovan sat up and took another swig of wine. 'Glad it measures up OK. I've always loved this place. Mum and I would come when I was a kid with a picnic in the holidays.'

'Just you two? Did your brother never come?' Somehow she couldn't stop probing—longing to know more about this man, his background and what made him tick.

Denovan shrugged. 'My father wasn't very interested in walking or views, and Frank...well, Frank was a lot older than me, and he and I didn't get on anyway...'

'Even when you were young?'

'Even then,' he remarked sadly. 'I suppose he regarded my mother as a usurper, coming into his life after he'd lost his mother. My father had remarried my mother very quickly and then I appeared—and perhaps that was a mistake.' His expression hardened. 'We never had what I'd call an idyllic family.'

Suddenly Kerry remembered the words of Nellie Styles, the old lady she'd visited before the flooding. She had mentioned the boys' animosity towards each other...and something else, but she couldn't remember quite what it was.

'It's a shame you've never made it up with Frank. He always seems quite laid back and he and I get on well. He's a good doctor.'

Denovan frowned. 'I'm sure he's a good doctor, but

you don't know him as intimately as I do,' he said
tersely. 'You make it sound as if we'd had a minor spat
but I can assure you it runs more deeply than a childhood difference, because in fact...' He stopped in mid-
sentence and looked at her guardedly.

'Because what?' she prompted.

He shook his head. 'Nothing. It's too complicated.'

Kerry bit her lip. She should have avoided the subject of his brother. 'Look, I'm sorry. It's nothing to
do with me, I know. I suppose I just wanted to know
more about your family. Frank never talks about the
past at all.'

'I'm not surprised Frank keeps his past to himself—
it doesn't make good listening, I'm afraid.' Denovan's
voice was bitter. 'You wouldn't believe me if I told you
the whole story anyway.'

'It's your past, not mine, Denovan. There's no need
to tell me,' she said gently, but she burned with curiosity to know the truth of the rift between the brothers, to know more about Denovan's mysterious other
life, which he so obviously wanted to keep to himself.

'Let's forget about him,' said Denovan in a lighter
tone. He leant over and topped up Kerry's cup with
more wine. 'You'd better finish this—after all, I'm
driving back in an hour or two so I'd best stick to one
glass.'

Kerry felt delightfully relaxed after some alcohol
racing through her on an empty stomach. The stress of
the past week seemed to evaporate as she rolled over
on her back on the mossy grass and looked up at the
canopy of trees over the little plateau they were on.

'Oh,' she murmured, 'this is heaven. I could just go
to sleep right here in the sun.'

The smile left Denovan's lips as he looked at Kerry's slender body lying so close to him. Slender but quite curvaceous, he thought gravely. She wasn't skinny with hip bones that stuck out, but had the kind of body it would be wonderful to feel against his—soft, warm, yielding. Her eyes were closed, her lips slightly parted and the urge to taste those soft lips was suddenly overwhelmingly tempting.

He sighed. The last person he should be fancying was his brother's colleague—how complicated would that be? It was extraordinary that he should even be working with Kerry with the bad history between him and Frank. Yet two weeks ago he had been in London and couldn't have imagined himself sitting on a grassy bank by Braxton Falls with a gorgeous girl like Kerry whom he'd only just met! He leaned nearer Kerry, still holding the paper cup in his hand, feasting on the softness of her skin, the way her cloud of dark hair framed her face.

A sudden babble of voices made Denovan look up as a party of hikers appeared, walking briskly down from the side of the waterfall. They gave him a friendly wave and disappeared down the valley path. He waved back at them, forgetting he was holding a cupful of wine in his hand.

'Eek! What was that?' Kerry gave a scream and sat bolt upright, brushing a stream of cold wine from her face.

'Hell…sorry… I waved with the wrong hand at those walkers! Oh, damnation, it's all over your T-shirt…' He made to dab the spill on her chest with a handkerchief he'd pulled out of his pocket. 'Let me dry it…'

She snatched the handkerchief and said quickly, 'It's OK. I can do that myself, thank you very much!'

There was laughter dancing in his eyes as he murmured, 'A pity...'

Kerry flicked a stern look at him before catching his eye and suddenly dissolving into giggles, and he laughed too as he watched her. Then gradually their laughter died away and they were staring at each other as if both had realised something momentous had occurred in those few moments. There was an almost palpable silence, the atmosphere electric with anticipation. Kerry began to breathe a little faster, her heart thumping uncomfortably in her chest. She was so close to him that she could see the thick lashes round those sexy, humorous eyes and the slight late-day stubble on his chin. Another second, she thought, and something was going to happen. Something she might regret.

Denovan broke the silence and leaned towards her, whispering, 'Kerry, you must know...'

With a great effort of will Kerry sprang to her feet and gave a forced laugh. 'Any more of that wine left?' she croaked. 'Or have you spilt it all?'

He got up slowly and raised a sardonic eyebrow. 'I might be able to find a few drops,' he remarked, his eyes still holding hers.

Denovan poured what was left into her plastic cup, and she turned away from him and sauntered casually away to lean against a tree, pretending to look at the view across the valley with her back to the falls, trying to calm her heart, which was beating like a demented drum against her ribs. There was no way anything could happen between them—Denovan was returning to London next week. She had to remember that. She could sense that he was very near her and she turned round brightly.

'We really ought to take this opportunity to have a discussion about the practice,' she said rather wildly, her voice breathless. 'I don't know if you've any more patient notes to load into the computer before you go?'

'Forget about the practice,' he said tersely. He put his hands on her shoulders, and looked into her hazel eyes. 'Kerry,' he said softly. 'What are you frightened of?'

She swallowed nervously. 'I don't know what you mean...' she faltered. She looked at her watch—her not-so-adroit change of subject hadn't worked. 'Perhaps we ought to be getting back. We've seen the falls and they're very beautiful, but it's going to take quite a while to walk back to the car.'

'We have plenty of time, and you haven't answered my question—what are you frightened of?' His grave face looked down at her and it was difficult to avoid his compelling gaze. 'You see,' he continued softly, 'I'm sure you wanted to kiss me then, just as much as I wanted to kiss you. Aren't I right? I know there was something electric between us a moment ago.'

Kerry took a deep breath, and said coolly, 'Denovan, don't be ridiculous. For goodness' sake, you've only been here a few days—I don't really know you at all. You're imagining things.'

He smiled and shook his head. 'I don't think so, Kerry—I know when there's a spark...'

Kerry felt a flash of irritation—he was so sure, so confident in his assumption that she was attracted to him, unable to think for a moment that she might *not* wish to kiss him!

'For goodness' sake, Denovan,' she snapped. 'I was

sceptical when your brother told me you were a womaniser—now I believe him!'

Denovan stepped back from her and said quietly, 'You think that, do you? You believe what Frank said, although you've admitted you don't know me very well?'

Kerry looked at him scornfully. 'Oh, I don't have to go by just what Frank said. You just have to look in most of the celebrity magazines to see you're featured with a bevy of beauties.'

Denovan's lips twitched and then he gave a roar of laughter. 'So that's it? Oh, Kerry, if you believe them, you'll believe anything!'

Kerry looked at him, rather nonplussed. 'What about Suzy de Forno, then?' she demanded, folding her arms. 'One magazine said you were practically engaged to her. And if you are, what are you doing making a pass at me?'

His blue eyes danced as he regarded her pugnacious figure. 'Suzy de Forno and I barely know each other—and I happen to know that she's actually engaged to a very nice guy who works in marketing.' He stepped towards her and, putting his arm round her waist, pulled her close to him, one hand tracing a delicate path across her jaw and down her neck. And Kerry felt her body respond instantly to that butterfly touch, and, angry with herself for being so pliant, she stiffened her body and turned her head away.

'A magazine photo doesn't mean anything, Kerry—you can make up any old caption for it,' he said. 'Those are just make-believe stories, but this is reality. Believe me, there's no one in my life at the moment and hasn't been for a long, long time. So I ask you again, what are you afraid of, sweetheart? After all, I was only going to give you a gentlemanly peck. Something just like this…'

And he leaned forward and brushed her lips with his. 'There!' he exclaimed. 'That wasn't so frightening, was it?'

His deep blue eyes danced at her and she found herself melting and trying to suppress a giggle. Denovan O'Mara might not want a lifelong commitment, but how wonderful it was to be desired by a drop-dead gorgeous guy after such a long time without anybody to love. And if he was free, why should she be afraid to let herself go a little with him?

Before she could reply, he leant towards her again, kissing her on her warm, soft, pliant mouth, not briefly as before but long and hard and passionately, and she didn't resist. His arms imprisoned her against the tree trunk and slowly her arms curved round his neck and pulled him against her. His mouth fluttered down to the little hollow in her neck, his hands caressing the soft swell of her breasts, and every nerve in her body tingled with anticipation, her limbs as pliant as jelly. This wasn't just a casual embrace—this was deliberate, exciting and mind-blowing!

Somewhere in the deep recesses of her mind she wondered if she was being a complete fool to allow… no, enjoy this man she'd known so briefly to make love to her—the man who not long ago she'd thought had been tough, unsympathetic, and who was leaving in two days' time. But she'd been lonely for too long and he was the first man since Andy who had made her pulse race. She sighed and gave in to the completely erotic pleasure of his touch on her body, his hard, demanding frame against hers, and she melted against him, never wanting this heaven to stop. She'd tried to resist him, but now she'd given in, and any problems there might be in the way of a relationship disappeared like gossamer in the wind.

CHAPTER SEVEN

THE sudden crack of thunder almost directly over their heads and a flash of lightning to the side of them was unexpected and terrifying. Kerry was still entwined in Denovan's arms, both of them blissfully relaxed, totally unprepared for the rapid darkening of the skies and the ominous drops of rain that started to fall.

She flinched and screamed, clutching Denovan. 'What's happened?'

Denovan hugged her to him and mumbled, 'It's OK, it's just a thunderstorm.'

'What do you mean, just a thunderstorm? We could get killed! We're under a tree, for heaven's sake!' She wriggled from him, stood up and grabbed her rucksack.

The drops of rain changed in an instant to a deluge, hitting them both with such force that in a few seconds they were completely soaked, as wet as if they'd been swimming.

Denovan took her hand and shouted over the noise of the storm, 'Perhaps you're right—we'd better take shelter. We'll go behind the waterfall. There's a cave there—we'll be safe until the storm blows over. Hang on to me!'

He bent down and scooped up his rucksack and

Kerry clung to him as inch by inch they managed to negotiate the slippery rocks on a ledge behind the cascade of water, all the time aware of the nearness of the lightning forking the ground too close to them for comfort, and the deafening crash of the thunder overhead. By the time they made the safety of the cave, their clothes were clinging to them and water was streaming down their bodies.

Denovan pushed back his dripping hair from his face and laughed, leaning against the wall of the cave. 'That's what happens when I kiss a girl,' he remarked with a smug grin. 'She feels as if she's been struck by a thunderbolt!'

Kerry wrinkled her nose at him and shook her head mock sternly—but it was only too true she admitted, still dizzy from his kisses a few minutes before. It had happened as suddenly as the thunderstorm—one minute they'd just been talking then, as if a switch had been thrown, the atmosphere between them had become charged, pulsating, and if this sudden storm hadn't burst on them, who knows what would have happened?

She looked down in comical dismay at her dripping trousers and T-shirt. 'Our clothes are wringing!'

'Perhaps we'd better take them off, then,' Denovan murmured, pulling off his shirt and throwing it over a rock in the corner of the cave. He turned towards her with dancing eyes. 'We don't want to catch pneumonia, do we?'

'Don't be ridiculous. Anyway, how are we going to dry them?' Kerry's voice was husky, trying not to look at his impressively muscled chest. 'We can't walk home with nothing on!'

'It'll stop raining in a minute and we can squeeze

them and hang them out for half an hour. I bet the sun will come out. And we both have cagoules in our rucksacks.'

'And what are we going to do for the next half-hour? I'm freezing!' she said, then bit her lip. She'd walked straight into that one as it was quite obvious that Denovan had plenty of ideas on that front!

He grinned wickedly at her and put his hands round her waist. 'I can think of plenty of things to warm us up,' he murmured, sliding his hands onto the bare flesh beneath her T-shirt. 'We were rudely interrupted a few minutes ago, just as we were getting to know each other better.'

Kerry laughed, but stepped back firmly and peered out through the cascade of water. The rain had almost stopped and just as suddenly as the storm had come it was moving away and blue sky and sunlight appeared in its wake. Perhaps it had been a blessing in disguise that the storm had come when it had—now she'd had time to pull herself together she realised what a fool she'd have been to have given in to the temptation that was Denovan. He was a temporary fixture, someone who'd admitted he wanted no ties, and probably looked on their liaison as a pleasurable interlude while he was in the area.

'We need to get going,' she said brusquely. 'I don't care how wet we are, it's not raining now. We have to pick up the car from the little railway and then you have to collect Archie.'

Denovan took her hand in his. 'Don't tell me this hasn't changed things,' he said softly.

Kerry's voice was as brisk as she could make it. 'It can't change things. You're going on Monday, for heaven's sake. You've another life…a wonderful job in London, and you don't want to work here. Better that we don't make too much of our…little liaison.'

The past few passionate minutes couldn't possibly have meant as much to Denovan as it had to her— perhaps in the circles in which he moved in London it was a normal occurrence. Sudden desolation filled her heart—she couldn't allow herself to hope that theirs would be a permanent love affair when he was going back so soon to his other life. The whole thing was fraught with difficulties. And after all it had just been a passionate kiss, nothing more!

'We must get back,' she repeated. 'Get into some dry clothes before we go and get Archie.'

Denovan took her arm and pulled her to him roughly. 'What the hell are you talking about—do you call what we just did "a little liaison"? We can't go back to where we were before—not…not after the past few minutes. I tell you, Kerry, that meant more to me than a "little liaison".'

Kerry shook her head. 'But your home and work is in London with Archie, and mine is here in Braxton. When Frank's better he'll be coming back to work here—how can we have a future?'

And all that was true, reflected Denovan. He was at the pinnacle of his job in London—that was why they were offering him another contract, something he had to decide about very soon. Most importantly, Archie needed stability, and at the moment Archie had a lovely childminder and a nursery school he enjoyed. Then he looked down at Kerry, at the curve of her cheek, the soft fullness of her lips and the remembrance of the passion between them a few minutes ago. Women like her came along very rarely. He had to think of something to keep them together.

'I'm not giving up on us before we've hardly started,' he said softly. 'Look, I'm going back to London on Tuesday, but I'll be coming back here to see you as soon as I can.' He held her against him, stroking her hair. 'I mean it, Kerry, you won't be able to keep me away. Let's take it one glorious step at a time and enjoy ourselves.'

Those were the sort of reassuring comments that just put off the evil day of decision—and how would that leave her? reflected Kerry rather bleakly. She was falling for a man who wasn't really available. It had probably been spur-of-the-moment passion on his side anyway. During the past weeks they'd each kept their distance, and suddenly in the space of an hour they'd started something passionate. And now there was no time left for them to get together alone. How could they build a solid foundation for their relationship after such a brief encounter? Then she flicked a look at Denovan's strong, sweet profile in the darkness of the cave and any sensible ideas of backing off from a relationship melted. At the moment, she decided, she'd go along with his suggestion. What had he said? One step at a time?

He hugged her to him again, and she knew when he held her close to him that there was no turning back for her. What had started that afternoon as a light-hearted kiss had become something that meant much more to her than that.

Denovan took her hand and squeezed it. 'Back to reality again, then. We'd better do something to make ourselves presentable.'

* * *

It had been a wonderful weekend and they'd had a happy Sunday with Archie, Kerry cooking a huge breakfast for them and in the afternoon going to show the little boy a farm with newborn lambs that he helped to feed. Afterwards he'd ridden on one of the little Shetland ponies the farmer kept.

Archie had been so excited and happy, clinging to both Denovan's and Kerry's hands, dragging them over to see the donkey that lived in the field with the ponies, roaring with laughter as a goose chased a duck for bread he'd thrown into the pond.

'I want to stay here for ever and ever,' he'd declared when they were leaving. 'This is my favourite place!'

'We'll come back very soon, I promise,' Denovan had said, and he'd smiled across at Kerry.

Kerry had smiled back, but she'd wondered if he'd be able to keep his promise.

'You look so much better than the end of last week!' exclaimed Daphne as she poured Kerry and Denovan a cup of coffee after they'd done the surgery on Monday morning. 'You were both dead on your feet on Friday afternoon—your outing on Saturday must have done you a lot of good.'

Kerry could feel Denovan's eyes boring into her back as he said enthusiastically. 'It certainly did, Daphne. I can't think when I've enjoyed a weekend more. And once again, thank you for looking after Archie, he didn't stop talking about the great time he had with you. I'm very grateful to you.'

'He's a dear little boy.' Daphne smiled. 'Didn't you find that walk up to the waterfall very exhausting? And you had to walk back soaking wet because of the rain. I can hardly manage to do anything energetic after I've climbed up!'

'Oh, we kept going quite well,' said Denovan, his voice smooth.

Kerry felt an urgent desire to giggle and she looked away from Denovan's dancing eyes. 'We did get pretty wet, but we sheltered in the cave for a while, so we were fine, thanks,' she said.

'Absolutely fine,' agreed Denovan solemnly, as he stirred two large spoonfuls of sugar into his coffee. 'It gave us a chance to discuss quite a few things.'

'That's good,' said Daphne comfortably. 'It's as well to know everything you can about the practice, even though you're only here until tomorrow.'

'I certainly think I know much more about things now.'

His steady glance held Kerry's for an intimate second, and her pulse rate bounded into rapid mode, as if he'd pressed an accelerator. Two days ago her relationship with Denovan had changed dramatically—it was no good pretending that they were just colleagues any more. Her passionate embrace with him still ran vividly through her mind, every moment precious and memorable. She'd known him for only a couple of weeks and now she couldn't get the man out of her mind!

Her emotions were like a see-saw, one minute filled with excited happiness and then, when she considered the episode more soberly, her excitement evaporated. She mustn't think of that afternoon as a prelude to a long-lasting relationship, she told herself sternly. Denovan would be gone to his other life in London tomorrow and soon she would probably be a fading memory for him.

Freda had been answering the phone, which seemed to ring continually as it usually did after the weekend. She swivelled round in her chair. 'There's an urgent call here—Nellie Styles's daughter, Betty, has just rung. She's up staying with her mother and when she came back from the shops she found Nellie on the floor, unable to move. The ambulance has got stuck in some deep mud in the valley on the way up and can't make it. Betty sounds distraught.'

'Oh, no, poor Nellie. I was hoping she'd improve now we had more help for her. I'll go at once,' said Kerry, pushing thoughts of Denovan firmly out of her head. She picked up her medical bag and turned to Denovan. 'She was the old lady I told you about who knew you as a small boy,' she explained.

'I remember her well. She used to cook for us all when we needed some help after my mother…well, that is, when we needed some help,' he amended. Then he added lightly, 'I'd like to see her again.'

Kerry flicked a look at her watch. 'If you can spare the time now, it might be a good idea if you could come with me. I'll need help to get Nellie off the floor if I have to take her to hospital myself in my car and I'd appreciate your input anyway.'

They walked briskly to Kerry's car and she continued to fill him in on Nellie's medical history.

'It might be a TIA. She's had a history of them over the past few months, although she's never had a true stroke.'

'How is her health otherwise?'

'She's very frail—she's recently been in hospital for a urinary tract infection. She's also very determined.

She was adamant she wouldn't go into hospital last time I saw her, but it may have to come to that.'

Nellie's daughter was standing at the door of the little house as they drove up, her hands clasped in agitation, looking anxiously up and down the road. It was obvious she'd been crying, and her face cleared in relief as they came in.

'Oh, thank goodness you're here,' she choked. 'I haven't known what to do. Poor Mum. When I came back from the shop, she couldn't seem to get the words out right and was just lying in a heap on the floor near the kitchen. I can't move her—she's a deadweight.'

She followed the two doctors into the house, twisting her hands together, her face distorted by worry. 'I'm sorry to be so jittery. It's just that Mum's always been such a strong character and it's horrible to see her laid so low.'

Kerry squeezed Betty's shoulder comfortingly, knowing the terrible panic and helplessness that Betty would feel. 'I know, Betty. You've had a terrible shock, but the main thing is you've got help quickly.' She turned to Denovan. 'This is my colleague, Dr O'Mara, who's been filling in for his brother for us. I thought it was a good idea to bring him along, too. Now, let's see how Nellie is, and perhaps you can answer some questions for us…' Her voice was brisk and no-nonsense, trying to bring things back to normality, to keep Betty composed in front of her mother.

Betty had put a pillow under Nellie's head and draped a blanket over her. Kerry bent down beside Nellie and smiled into the old lady's pale, frightened eyes.

'Hello, Nellie, how did you manage to fall, then? Did you trip or just feel very dizzy?'

'Dizzy,' said Nellie after a few moments of working her mouth. 'I'm OK,' she said after another pause, finding difficulty in forming words. Then she clutched Kerry's hand and looked at her imploringly. 'Don't... Not hospital...'

'Let's just see how you are, Nellie. Look, I've brought someone with me that you knew from a long time ago—do you remember him?'

Denovan squatted down beside her. 'I was only a lad when you came to cook for my father and Frank and me. I loved your hot scones with the home-made jam you made!'

Nellie stared up at him, and gradually a smile appeared on her lined face. 'Denovan...young tearaway!' She lifted her frail hand and clutched his arm. 'Eh... good...good boy!'

Kerry slipped a cuff round the old lady's arm and began to take her blood pressure. 'Fancy you recognising him after all these years—that's a pretty good effort!'

Nellie actually chuckled, a mischievous sparkle returning to her eyes. 'Still...very handsome!'

'You'll be making him big-headed,' remarked Kerry with a grin, unwinding the cuff. 'BP's a bit low—one hundred and five over seventy,' she murmured to Denovan. She looked up at Betty standing rigidly with her hands to her mouth. 'Does your mother's speech sound any better than when you first came back?'

Betty brushed a tear from her eye and nodded. 'Yes...much better. At least she's saying something— she couldn't say anything before, although she was trying to. Is she going to be all right, Doctor?'

'Hopefully she'll be feeling better very soon. Why

don't you go and put on the kettle and we'll have a nice cup of tea?'

Oh, the wonderful calming effects of making tea and drinking it when there was a crisis! Betty trotted off with alacrity, already feeling more in command of herself by doing something constructive.

'What do you think, Denovan?' asked Kerry.

'Nellie's speech has obviously been affected, but it's not very marked dysphasia. I think it's transient and she's getting it back,' he said thoughtfully. 'Her limb movement seems OK. I guess you're right and she's had a slight TIA. Let's see what her swallowing reflex is like and then perhaps give her an aspirin to dissolve any clot.'

'Fine. Can we get her in a sitting position first?'

Denovan pushed a chair behind Nellie and between them they managed to prop her up against the seat of the chair with a cushion behind her back. The colour had come back into the old lady's cheeks and she looked at the two doctors in a resigned way.

'So...am I going to live?' she said slowly.

'Of course you are! Just take a sip of water for us.'

'Water?' said Nellie with spirit. 'I want some tea and a biscuit!'

It was obvious that Nellie was improving rapidly and Kerry laughed. 'Have the water first, Nellie—we just want to make sure you can swallow it properly. We don't want you choking!'

Betty returned with a tray of tea and biscuits, looking in a frightened way at her mother as if expecting her to expire any moment. She put the tray down and Kerry got up from Nellie's side and drew Betty slightly away from the patient.

'It's all right, Betty,' she said reassuringly. 'We think your mother's had what we call a TIA or transient is-chaemic attack, which is when an artery supplying blood to the brain becomes temporarily blocked.'

'How do you know that's what it is?'

'We can't know absolutely until tests are done,' said Denovan gently. 'But all your mother's symptoms point to that—a very sudden attack of dizziness and dis-turbance of speech, which starts to come back fairly soon. But we're going to take Nellie to hospital for a check-up.'

'I told you I don't want to go to hospital!' Nellie's voice had surprising strength in it—she'd obviously picked up the word 'hospital'.

'Come on, Nellie, it's unlikely you'll be in overnight, but we've got to make sure we know what's going on.' Denovan turned his most persuasive and sweet smile on her and Nellie subsided with a sigh.

'You doctors, all bullies…' she murmured.

There was a knock at the front door and two burly men in paramedic uniform appeared.

'Hello, there! Sorry we're late. We had to get a farmer to pull us out of the mud at the bottom there. There's still so much mud about. Now, how's the pa-tient?'

Kerry quickly filled him in on Nellie's history, re-lieved that she wouldn't have to take her to hospital herself. It was much better to be transported by an am-bulance with all the equipment in it to help Nellie—oxygen, monitoring of her blood and her reactions.

'I'm sure you want to go with your mother, Betty,' said Kerry. 'Why don't you get together her night things and toiletries…just in case she has to stay in?'

Nellie didn't hear her last remark as she was too busy trying to tell the paramedics that she was absolutely fine and it was ridiculous that she was going near a hospital.

'You do as you're told,' Denovan instructed her, mock severely. 'That's what you used to tell me when I was young.'

Nellie smiled at him as she was taken out in a wheelchair to the ambulance. 'Cheeky thing,' she mumbled. 'You got a girl yet, young man? About time you did…' She grinned wickedly and pointed to Kerry. 'You won't find a prettier lass around than Dr Latimer…get on with it, lad!'

This time her speech came out as clear as a bell and Denovan flicked a mischievous glance at Kerry. 'I'll work on that advice, Nellie!' He grinned.

'Mum!' said Betty in shocked tones. 'You mustn't say that!'

Then Nellie and Betty went off in the ambulance, and Denovan put his arm round Kerry as they watched the vehicle disappear down the road.

'Still happy?' he asked, looking down at her with that sweet smile and hugging her against him.

'Whoa!' She laughed. 'We need to be a bit discreet, Denovan, especially in a small place like this. People will be talking!'

'Who cares? Does it matter that we're rather fond of each other?'

'Let's not broadcast the fact, that's all,' she said lightly. 'You'll be gone tomorrow and who knows? You may decide to take up that new contract for television work.'

He looked at her gravely. 'Suppose I did—suppose

the terms were so incredible that it would be difficult to refuse? Why don't you think about working in London? You'd easily get a job, and we could be together.'

It was a tempting thought, and rather exciting. She'd be able to go out with Denovan properly then, with no small community following their every move or a disapproving Frank nearby. She'd be a completely free agent. She almost laughed at the thought—how mad was that, to hare off to an unknown future in the hope that after one passionate kiss her relationship with Denovan might be permanent?

Kerry looked down the little main street of Braxton. It still looked a muddy mess, and many houses still stood empty even a couple of weeks after the flood. So much still to be done, so many lives disrupted, businesses ruined. Whatever her dilemmas, thought Kerry resolutely, the village people were going through a crisis with worries much worse than hers, and she would do her level best to help them.

She shook her head. 'No, Denovan, I can't do that. I love Braxton and the people here. They've been so kind to me, especially since Andy died. I'm going to do all I can to help them and try and repay some of their kindness—they deserve that at least. I feel I belong here. Do you understand?'

He hugged her to him. 'You're right—why should I suggest you leave this beautiful part of the world because of me? And what did I say before? I'm not going to give up on you, Kerry. And I'm taking you out tonight. It'll be somewhere special so I've asked Daphne to babysit. And it won't be a "farewell" dinner, just a taste of things to come, I hope!'

And she laughed up at him, her heart leaping with

the prospect of a romantic evening with Denovan—and yet her happiness was mixed with a flickering doubt that he might seem to have a better future in London than in Braxton Falls.

CHAPTER EIGHT

KERRY looked doubtfully at her reflection in the mirror. Was the coral silk dress she'd bought for her cousin's wedding a little over the top for a meal out in the country? She adjusted the straps slightly—perhaps it revealed more cleavage than she remembered, but she knew the vibrant colour suited her, and she wanted to look every bit as glamorous as the women Denovan was used to dating in London, didn't she? Why shouldn't she pull all the stops out for the first proper date she'd been on for over a year with a gorgeous guy she might not see again?

She gave a little twirl, liking the feel of the fluted skirt as it rippled out around her legs, and a little shiver of excitement whipped through her—for once she had something to dress up for! She bent nearer the mirror to check on her make-up and added a touch of blusher to her cheeks and a quick spray of perfume on her wrists.

In the mirror her eyes looked large, sparkling with excitement and something else—perhaps anticipation? She was only too aware that a man like Denovan wasn't going to be satisfied with a passionate kiss at the end of the evening—after what had happened two days ago they both knew that there was a sexual tension between them that could only lead one way. Would she go along with that? She wanted to, of course. More than anything in the whole world she longed to be made love to by Denovan—and probably, she reminded herself, so did many, many other women! Was she going to allow that to happen knowing that this might be the first and last time he took her out?

She frowned into the mirror as if her reflection would give her the answer. Should she go with the flow and enjoy her time with Denovan while it lasted, or was she risking her heart falling for a playboy doctor? Then just as she started to put in her favourite pair of drop earrings, the doorbell rang.

'Who can that be? Whoever it is I hope they don't take too long about it,' Kerry muttered crossly.

Denovan had taken Archie round to Daphne's house as the little boy had pleaded to stay with them the night so he could play with their trains, and Denovan was due back any minute to take her out to the restaurant. With an impatient sigh she ran down the stairs and went to answer the door, hoping it wasn't a medical emergency—one of the drawbacks about living in the centre of the village was that she was far too accessible! She opened the front door then stared with incredulity at the frail figure on the door step.

'F-Frank!' she stuttered. 'What on earth are you doing here? I thought they were going to keep you in for a few more days?'

He shook his head. 'I feel much better and I'm sick of lounging about in the hospital so I decided to take a taxi home and it's waiting for me now, but I wanted to see you first. I'm only staying for a minute.' His eyes travelled over her glamorous dress. 'Wow!' he said appreciatively. 'You look wonderful. What's the occasion?'

'Don't stand on the doorstep, Frank, for goodness' sake. Come in.' Kerry stood to one side and he stepped past her into the little living room.

Frank sat down on one of the chairs. 'You haven't answered me. Is there something special on?'

'I've been asked out to dinner, so I thought I'd wear the dress I was going to wear at the wedding in Tobago.'

'Oh, Kerry, I'm sorry about that. Because of my accident you had to cancel, didn't you?'

'It's not important—the main thing is that you're back on the road to recovery.' She looked at him sternly. 'You're not thinking of working yet, I hope?'

'That's what I needed to speak to you about,' Frank said. 'I realise I must give it a little while longer to work full time yet, but you can't carry the burden all yourself.'

'I can manage...'

'Denovan's going back tomorrow, isn't he? I imagine you'll miss his help. Has he managed to slot in OK?'

'We've worked well together—and the patients like him very much.'

'Oh, yes,' said Frank lightly, and with a smile to soften his words, 'I can imagine he's gone down a storm with our female patients. Denovan always has a host of groupies following him, like bees round a honey pot really.' He laughed. 'I believe he's quite a ladies' man. I expect that's one of the reasons he's become such a celebrity.'

It was true, thought Kerry wryly. Denovan was gorgeous, and it was no good assuming that he'd lead the life of a monk when he returned to London.

'Everyone likes him, Frank, not just the women!'

'You've not been tempted yourself, then?' asked Frank with a teasing grin.

Kerry hoped the blush that she felt rising in her face wasn't too apparent—obviously Frank was just trying to rib her, but she wasn't going to admit to him that she had feelings for Denovan, too!

She ignored his remark and said briskly, 'Actually, it's been a great relief to have someone here to help out. Now, how about a cup of tea? And what about your house? If you'd told me you were coming home I'd have stocked up your fridge for you and put the heating on.'

'That's kind of you, but I managed to get in touch with my cleaner and she's got the house ready. I really came round to put a suggestion to you. How about if I were to come in for two hours every day?'

'Don't be silly, Frank, it's only two weeks since your operation…'

Frank held up his hand. 'Hear me out, Kerry. I need something to do. I can't bear lolling about the house all day without a purpose. At least I'll be able to sort out the paperwork, see the occasional patient perhaps— nothing too taxing. And I really do feel so much better.'

'I think it's most unwise…'

There were sounds of footsteps outside and then the front door opened and Denovan came in. He stopped short when he saw Frank, his smile fading from his face, but his voice was reasonably civil when he spoke.

'So you're back! I certainly didn't expect you to be discharged yet,' he observed.

'Oh, I'm well on the road to recovery—back to normal. I'm not spending any more time in hospital so I discharged myself,' said Frank equably.

'Don't you think that's rather foolish?' exclaimed Denovan bluntly. 'Your head's had a hell of a battering.'

Frank laughed. 'I know what I'm doing, Denovan. Anyway, I believe you're leaving tomorrow? Back to being a celebrity hot-shot doc, I suppose? I dare say you've missed all the attention you get in London in a little place like Braxton.'

Although his tone was light and inoffensive, Kerry looked at Denovan, wondering if he would rise to his brother's teasing. Denovan's face darkened, his fists bunched hard in his pockets.

'What do you mean by that, Frank?' he growled. 'I haven't missed London. I've enjoyed my time here— but I can tell it's time to go back now you're on the scene.'

'Don't go back on my account, dear brother,' said Frank smoothly. 'I believe you've done an excellent job here. Charmed everyone as usual!'

Denovan's eyes glinted dangerously. 'Don't patronise me, please!'

'I'm not!' protested Frank. 'I'm very grateful to you for helping out.'

Kerry looked from one man to the other. Although Frank had been very pleasant to all intents and purposes, she could feel the tension between them, especially from Denovan. Suddenly the atmosphere seemed to crackle with hostility and to Kerry's eyes it looked as if the brothers were almost enjoying sparring with each other, winding each other up.

She stepped forward and said lightly, 'Now, Denovan, I'm sure Frank wasn't patronising you.'

Denovan whipped round. 'Please don't enter into it,' he snapped. 'I know very well what Frank's implying.'

Kerry stared at him, her mouth open. The charming Denovan had disappeared and in his place was the dour, taciturn man she'd first spoken to on the phone after Frank's accident.

She shrugged. 'I just don't understand why you're at daggers drawn with your brother—and I don't want to know. I just think it's a pity that you can't forgive and forget whatever it was that happened between you.'

'I can never forget what he did,' snarled Denovan.

Frank's benign expression changed, and his eyes became cold. 'Always harking back, aren't you? But, then, you always were a mummy's boy!' he said mockingly. 'To be honest, your mother was no better than she should have been...'

There was a stunned silence, except for Kerry's horrified intake of breath.

'How dare you say that?' said Denovan, his voice dangerously quiet. 'My mother made mistakes, sure, but she was unhappy.'

'You always blame me, Denovan—I'm no saint, but it's about time you stopped accusing me of ruining your life. Get over it, for God's sake!'

The two men glared angrily at each other, their fists clenched, and Denovan stepped forward as if to punch his brother. Any minute now, thought Kerry, they'd be literally at each other's throats! She put her hand up as she stepped between them and looked at them severely.

'Will you two listen to yourselves? Stop hurting each other like this! You should be utterly ashamed, both of you, behaving like street kids. It's appalling.'

Denovan shrugged and stepped back, and Kerry took a deep breath.

'Frank didn't come to rile you, Denovan—he merely came to say he'd do a few hours a week to help out until he's stronger. It's not what I'd advise, but he knows all the implications as much as we do—and if he really wants to, I'm grateful. And now I'll go and make some tea.'

Frank stood up. 'Not for me, thanks, Kerry. My taxi's waiting.' His gaze flickered over Denovan's tall figure, dressed in an open-necked white shirt and jacket and lightweight trousers, and he added with a tight smile, 'And you're obviously the person taking Kerry out to dinner now. Where are you off to?'

'The Farmer's Plough,' said Denovan dourly.

Frank looked from him to Kerry and raised an eyebrow, then nodded slowly. 'Ah…I see. Very upmarket. Well…have a good evening. I'll speak to you tomorrow, Kerry.'

He gave a brief nod to Denovan and went out.

There was a short silence then Kerry observed angrily, 'You acted like a schoolboy—can't you try and behave together? I know you feel he's done you a great wrong, but—'

'You know nothing about the situation between us,' rasped Denovan, his eyes bright with anger.

'Maybe I don't,' retorted Kerry, 'but at least remember Frank's been seriously ill.'

That familiar closed look came over Denovan's face and he replied stonily, 'And he's a fool to discharge himself so early.'

'Well, I suppose he knows how he feels—and he was good enough to offer to help me out a bit.'

Denovan raised an eyebrow. 'If he thinks he can help, he damn well ought to. He's put you to a lot of inconvenience.'

Kerry sighed—there seemed no way he could be reconciled with his brother, and she didn't want to spoil an evening she'd been looking forward to so much by bickering. *Oh, dear,* she thought crossly, *we've started off the evening on the wrong foot.* She looked at Denovan's thunderous face and wondered how they were going to get through the next two hours in a pleasant manner.

'Look,' she said crisply, her eyes sparking angrily across at him, 'if you'd rather not go out tonight after all, that's fine by me—but I certainly don't want to sit in front of an angry man for the rest of the evening. I know you brothers have some sort of issue between you, and you may not think it's any of my business, but frankly it affects me inasmuch as it makes you disgracefully bad-tempered!'

Denovan scowled. 'So you think it's all my fault, do you? I'm to blame, despite Frank making the most crass remarks?'

'Yes,' conceded Kerry. 'What he said about your mother was very hurtful. But he's been ill—you don't try and hit a man who's just come out of hospital, for heaven's sake,' she snapped. 'Besides, he's always been perfectly pleasant to me—I can't imagine why you rile each other so. Even when I first rang you up to tell you about his accident, you were incredibly unsympathetic.'

'Then perhaps I should tell you,' growled Denovan. 'Stop you jumping to the most unfair conclusions.'

Kerry looked at him icily. 'Perhaps you should. At

the moment it all seems so childish and completely inexplicable, scoring points off each other like juveniles.'

They stared at each other angrily, a brief silence between them, and Kerry bit her lip, suddenly wondering how it had come to this—two people who'd exchanged the most passionate kisses two days before now shouting at each other so angrily. Denovan brushed a hand through his hair in exasperation, leaving it standing in rough spikes over his head.

'Oh, hell,' he muttered, 'it all happened a long time ago now.'

'What did?'

He was silent for a second or two, looking down at the floor as if psyching himself up to tell her, then he looked at Kerry directly and said bluntly, 'If you really want to know why Frank and I fell out, I'll tell you. Many years ago, your precious Frank seduced my young, vulnerable mother. My father found out and, ashamed and terrified, she fled from home. I never saw her again.' His voice was harsh. 'There! Does that convince you that I have some reason to dislike my dear half-brother?'

For a moment or two Kerry could find no words in response as she gazed at Denovan in horror. Eventually she stammered, '*F-Frank? Frank* seduced your mother? How do you know?'

'After my father's death I was going through his papers and I found his journal—it was all written down meticulously there.'

Kerry looked at him mutely, devastated for the young Denovan, never seeing his mother again, and learning about her infidelity with his half-brother.

Denovan watched her expression and sighed. 'Oh, I

didn't know at the time it happened, of course—I was ten years old and was told that my parents had split up because my mother had had to leave. You can imagine how that rocked my world. I was a very sad young boy during my school days. I did have one letter from my mother saying that she would come back one day, but that never happened…'

His voice drifted away, his sad words hanging in the air, poignant, tragic. Kerry shook her head, hardly able to believe what she was hearing. She looked compassionately at his sad face, half-shadowed in the small room. 'Oh, Denovan,' she said softly. 'I'm so sorry.'

'Do you really want to hear this sob story?' Denovan said wearily. 'It doesn't show my family in a very good light, I'm afraid.'

'But you must tell me,' said Kerry, putting a hand on his arm. 'It'll help me understand why you and Frank seem to be at each other's throats.'

He sighed and started to pace the floor. 'Very well… My mother was very young when she had me—barely twenty years old—and it was soon obvious that the marriage was a disaster. She had been my father's receptionist and I suppose she saw marriage to the village GP as a step up in her humdrum life. After my father's first wife died I guess he was lonely, and although I suppose he loved my mother in his way, they didn't have a happy marriage.'

'Oh, my,' breathed Kerry, dumbfounded by the story. She sat down on the sofa abruptly. 'It's the most tragic story.'

'My unhappy mother was looking for comfort and perhaps she thought she'd found it with Frank. OK, she was a bit older than he was, but her confidence had been shattered by my father. Frank started an affair with her, then dumped her when our father found out.' Denovan's expression was stony. 'It's no good crying about it. I don't think I've ever told anyone before… it all seemed so sordid, something to keep to oneself. It's something I try and forget, but when I see Frank, it brings it all back.'

Kerry shook her head and said gently, 'Where Frank's concerned, it's still very raw. Perhaps it helps to talk about it.'

'Maybe you're right.'

'I suppose Frank's nose was pushed severely out of joint when you came along—he'd lost his own mother and he resented the new baby and woman in his father's life,' suggested Kerry.

'Perhaps,' admitted Denovan. 'But we never got on—the incident with my mother was just a climax to our bad feeling for each other.' He leaned back against the wall and folded his arms, looking down at Kerry sardonically.

'So there you have it,' he said matter-of-factly. 'The saga of the O'Mara family. When I discovered the truth in Dad's journal years later, I confronted Frank and I'm afraid the resulting row left scars between us that have never healed and probably never will. You see, I had to stand up for my mother whatever the circumstances.'

'I…I don't know what to say,' said Kerry at last. 'The Frank I know as a colleague is easy to work with and works hard himself. I feel sorry that both of you had an unhappy past, but you were young then and surely you aren't going to let this hatred you both feel for each other destroy the rest of your lives?'

'It's so hard to brush it aside, Kerry, but perhaps

one day we'll manage to bury our differences. I guess Frank and I've been at each other's throats so long that we don't realise the impact it has on everyone else— we've got used to it.'

'So no chance of you coming back to Braxton Falls, then?' she said lightly.

He hesitated for a moment, fiddling with his watch strap. 'I love Braxton, but it would be difficult—you can see that, can't you?'

Then he put his hands on Kerry's shoulders, looking down at her with those amazing blue eyes of his that made thinking of anything else but his electric presence impossible.

'Look, sweetheart,' he said softly, 'let's start the evening again, shall we? I'm sorry about what happened with Frank and I just now. I don't want to think about him at the moment. You're a much more interesting subject to me right now. I want to concentrate on you. You look absolutely delectable and if I wasn't so hungry I'd suggest we didn't bother with any food tonight. Please don't let's spoil our last night together.'

Their last night together. It sounded so final, something over before it had hardly begun. She couldn't let Denovan leave on a sour note, thought Kerry—she wanted their last meeting to be a happy one. Even the light touch of his hands on her shoulders sent a tremor through her body, and the tension between them melted away. She stood up and took Denovan's arm, smiling up at him.

'Let's get going, then,' she said. 'I'm starving.'

The Farmer's Plough was only a five-minute walk away from Kerry's cottage. It stood at the top of a hill overlooking the village and the pretty valley with its patch-work of fields, an old barn converted into a restaurant. Oak beams criss-crossed the high ceiling and there were cosy tables in intimate little alcoves around the walls, while bigger tables occupied the centre of the room. Soft golden lights on the tables gave the whole place a warm and cosy feel, and in one corner a pianist played softly by a small dance floor.

'This is lovely, Denovan,' murmured Kerry, look-ing round the room with pleasure, suddenly feeling her mood lifting. 'Who told you about it?'

He grinned. 'I asked Daphne where she thought I could take you for a farewell meal. She said this was the best place in the area, though it's not long been open.'

They were led to one of the little alcoves, where a waiter pulled out chairs for them and with a flourish placed napkins on their laps.

'I feel this is our own private little room.' Kerry smiled.

Denovan looked at her covertly as she studied the menu. In the glow from the table lamp Kerry's soft skin looked peachy cream, and the curve of her full breasts under the neckline of her dress was tantalising. She looked a knock-out in that sexy dress! He took a deep breath and tried to concentrate on choosing some food for himself. This time next week he'd be in London, plunging back into life in the fast lane, possibly back on a new television show with a juicy contract to go with it. How different from the past two weeks in the idyllic countryside of Braxton, working alongside one of the most beautiful women he'd ever met. He remem-bered how reluctant he'd been to come back—and how surprisingly happy he'd been while he'd been working in Braxton. He was going to miss Kerry very much—it wouldn't be easy, adjusting to life without her.

He had ordered champagne and the waiter poured it into their two glasses. Denovan raised his glass. 'To the future,' he said with a smile. 'It's been a great two weeks, especially this last weekend!'

'To the future,' agreed Kerry, but a shiver of sadness flickered through her. 'I hope it all works out for you in London—and I really want to thank you for your help over the past two weeks. I couldn't have managed without you.'

'I was glad to help.' He paused for a second, holding his wine glass up to the light and letting the bubbles swirl round, then smiled at her again. 'Actually, I should be thanking you. I've enjoyed being back in general practice, even if there has been a lot of water around!'

Kerry felt her heart turn over. When he smiled so engagingly he looked so gorgeous. His eyes danced and held hers, sending a familiar flash of response through her body. It wasn't fair, she thought mournfully, that a man she liked so much should be vanishing from her life when she was just getting to know him. And now she knew the story behind the two brothers' antipathy towards each other, she supposed there was no chance that Denovan would want to come back to Braxton. She would miss him so much—and also little Archie, with his mischievous ways. How quiet her world would seem without them.

In the background the piano was playing a rather dreamy, romantic tune and their eyes locked over the table. Were they thinking the same thing? Kerry wondered. Was this evening to be a prelude to something more permanent or, as she suspected, the finale to something that had only just started? Would this be their first and last date? Denovan watched the grave expression on her face, and as if he'd read her thoughts stood up and held out his hand. 'Cheer up, Kerry,' he murmured. 'You've got to work for your supper. Let's have a dance.'

He pulled her closely to him and put his face to hers—and she forgot about being gloomy, because her body was pressed to the hard wall of his chest. It was heavenly to feel the beat of his heart against hers, the slight roughness of his chin against her cheek, his hand firmly in the small of her back, as they swayed silently together to the gentle rhythm of the music.

But even through the longing of desire as they danced, Kerry decided firmly that this was as far as it should go. Frank's words about Denovan being known as a ladies' man stuck in her mind, so although every nerve in her body was responding like a light switch to his fizzing sexiness, on no account was she going to finish the evening by going to bed with Denovan, only to be just another conquest in his busy social life when he left for London!

It was a cool night, but the sky was clear and like a velvet cloth sparkling with myriad stars. It had been a lovely evening after all, and it had passed very quickly—too quickly, thought Kerry ruefully. She couldn't stop thinking as the evening progressed that it was Denovan's last night, and there was only an hour or two left with just the two of them together.

They held hands as they sauntered down the hill

and past the little shops, some of them still boarded up after the floods.

'It doesn't seem that it was such a short time ago that we rescued Sirie from the fallen bridge,' Denovan commented. 'So much has happened since then.'

It was hard to believe that then she hadn't known Denovan at all, reflected Kerry, whereas now she knew so much about his sad background and the circumstances that had torn his family apart. No wonder he was wary of having a serious commitment after his experience with the women in his life—he'd been let down too many times.

Denovan slipped his arm round her shoulders and smiled down at her as they went up the path to the cottage. 'How about a nightcap before we go up?' he suggested.

Kerry swallowed hard—this was where she would be very firm and say a brisk goodnight then march up to bed, she thought. She turned the key in the front door without answering, and he bent down and kissed the nape of her neck.

They stepped through the door and Denovan pulled her towards him before she could get to the safety of the stairs.

'How lovely that for once we're alone,' he murmured. 'With no one to interrupt us.' He put his hands on her hair and pulled out the pins that held it in its chignon so that it tumbled in disarray round her shoulders. 'Ah,' he said in satisfaction. 'I've been longing to do that all evening.'

Kerry put up a hand to push her hair back. 'You... you shouldn't have done that,' she said reprovingly.

Denovan laughed. 'Why not? You look sensational with your hair down.'

Then he held her at arm's length for a few seconds, his eyes sweeping over her. 'Oh, Kerry,' he said huskily, 'you are utterly beautiful. We've had so short a time together.'

She wanted to cry out, *Then stay here! Stay with me—forget London!* But she couldn't bring herself to do it.

He bent his head and his lips touched hers softly at first, then more passionately, moving down her neck with the softest of butterfly kisses. A heady, disorientated feeling swept through Kerry—her good resolutions seemed to be dissolving rapidly.

It was crazy. Denovan was leaving Braxton and might never return, and however much she longed to be desired and loved again, she mustn't give in. It would be too easy at this moment to capitulate completely.

'I've got a busy day tomorrow—I must get a good night's sleep,' she said breathlessly, pulling away from him.

He dropped his arms to his sides and nodded. 'Of course…and I've got an early start, so perhaps we'd better turn in.'

Their eyes met and held in the silence of the room, and then, as she'd known he would, he moved towards her again and put his arms round her, and suddenly she didn't care if he wasn't looking for commitment and that he was going back to London the next day. She wanted him now and to hell with the consequences.

'I've been wanting to do this all evening,' whispered Denovan. 'I know we only have such a short time…'

His voice trailed off as he nuzzled into her neck, then gently he pulled her down onto the floor.

'I thought we were going to have an early night?' teased Kerry.

'Change of plan,' he said with a grin.

Then gently he peeled the straps of the coral dress from her shoulders—and she did nothing to stop him, just watched as he tossed his jacket to one side and tore off his shirt. He propped himself up on his arms, looking down at her with his startling blue eyes dark with desire.

'I truly didn't think the evening would end like this,' he whispered. 'But it sort of seems a fitting way to say *adieu.*'

'A perfect way,' breathed Kerry.

She stretched her limbs under him, luxuriating in his strong-muscled frame on hers, every nerve in her body seeming to tingle with anticipation. Had she ever felt this powerful explosion of passion with Andy? Unfair, unfair to judge. She couldn't think of that. She was with Denovan now, so skilled at arousing her to a fever-pitch of desire, his hands exploring her most secret places, his own craving for her only too obvious.

He drew her to him and said throatily, 'My beautiful, fiery Kerry—how wonderful is this?'

And afterwards, as he held her in his arms, she felt a marvellous sense of release, of letting the past go. From now on she'd look to the future—and surely, after what had just happened, it had to include Denovan. This couldn't be the end of the story, could it?

As if in answer to her unspoken question, he brushed away the strands of hair that had fallen across her forehead, and looked deep into her eyes. 'Don't let this be goodbye,' he murmured. 'Let's just say it's a work in progress!'

CHAPTER NINE

How quiet the cottage seemed! And no toy cars lying about, ready to send her flying when she stepped on them, no shirts festooning the rail in the bathroom, only one coffee cup on the drainer by the sink in the kitchen. Kerry looked mournfully around at the empty room. Denovan and Archie had left the day before for London, and she felt a horrible void of loneliness.

It was only two nights since the momentous revelations about the brothers' past had been disclosed. It had been a bad start to an evening she'd been so excited about, and then miraculously it had improved beyond all imagination! In her mind's eye she recalled the way Denovan had looked at her in the restaurant, the way he'd held her when they'd danced, but most of all the end of the evening when they'd made such passionate and wild love.

Had she made the biggest mistake in her life, making love to a man who'd said he didn't want a permanent relationship? Too late, she thought wryly. She had done and now she couldn't help wondering if she was joining a long line of his ex-girlfriends.

She'd had a phone call from Denovan when he'd arrived in London to say that he'd been offered a big contract to appear daily on a talk show where he'd be required to interview people and comment on health issues. He was excited about the prospect because it seemed to involve more than his previous work—and the salary was huge! He begged Kerry to come and see him the following weekend.

'I'm so sorry, Denovan, I'm busy this weekend and my mother may come up some time. She wants to tell me about my cousin's wedding.'

'Pity. I thought we could celebrate my new job—if I finally decide to accept it,' he said.

Gloomily Kerry wondered if she would feel like celebrating something that would anchor him even more firmly in London. And next Saturday would be her birthday. Somehow celebrating that by herself didn't seem any fun at all.

She sipped her breakfast coffee, now grown cold, and gazed unseeingly across the kitchen. She felt in limbo, not sure of Denovan's feelings for her and yet certain that when they were together they clicked like two pieces in a jigsaw. Then gradually the clock on the wall swam into focus, and to her horror revealed that it was nearly eight o'clock! Her first patient would be in at eight-thirty. She grabbed her coat and bag and ran out of the house to the surgery.

'So how was your evening at the Farmer's Plough?' Frank O'Mara had come into her room as she was reading through the emails on her computer before she started her working day. 'Did it live up to expectations?'

'Yes, oh, yes, it was lovely, thank you.'

Kerry tried to sound composed, but the mention of

her night with Denovan made her heartbeat rocket. Of course it hadn't been just lovely—it had been sensational, and far beyond her expectations.

Frank sat on the side of the desk, watching her face. 'Denovan always knew how to give a girl a good time,' he remarked blandly. 'I suppose he'll be coming back to see you in Braxton?'

'I've no idea, Frank.' Kerry's voice was cold—she was a little irritated by Frank's frequent allusions to Denovan's prowess with women. 'I believe he may be offered a very good job on one of the TV channels so he probably won't have time.'

'Perhaps you'll go and see him?'

'What? Oh, I don't know. There's lots to do here at the moment.'

Frank nodded, smiling. 'Oh, well, back to business as usual.' He stood up from the desk and said briskly, 'Right, I think we should look into getting a permanent part-time partner—we're going to need someone else even when I come back full time, what with the new housing estate up the road pushing up the patient numbers. I'd like a meeting at the end of next week to discuss that and other matters if that's OK with you?'

'Of course. It's about time we reviewed things. I haven't had time for the administration aspect of the practice lately.'

Kerry was glad he'd got off the subject of Denovan and on to the concerns of the practice. She felt on easier ground when she was talking to Frank about work and not her private life. They'd always had a cordial business relationship, but except for drinks with the rest of the staff at Christmas or New Year didn't see each other socially. He was much older than her and had been married until an acrimonious divorce a year ago. Frank turned at the door before he left the room. 'By the way,' he said casually, 'if you're free this weekend, I'd like to take you out for dinner—just a little thank-you for all you've done for me while I've been in hospital.'

Kerry looked at him, startled, and for some reason a little uncomfortable at the thought of an evening by herself with Frank. It may have been many years ago when he was a young man that the incident between him and Denovan's mother had occurred, and it probably hadn't been all his fault, nevertheless, Denovan felt Frank had ruined his life—she'd feel a little awkward going out to dinner with his half-brother.

'Oh, really, Frank, there's no need to entertain me. As long as you're feeling better, that's reward enough. And actually my mother's coming over on Sunday with some friends.'

'What about Saturday night, then?' Frank persisted, then put his hand up as if to pre-empt anything Kerry might say. 'Please! I'd like to—it's only a small thanks for carrying on so gallantly when I was fool enough to injure myself.'

Kerry sighed inwardly. For some reason she felt flat, not in the mood for going out—especially not with Frank.

He looked at her assessingly as if trying to read her thoughts, then said lightly, 'I hope you're not prejudiced against me. Whatever Denovan said, I don't seduce young women, you know. It really wasn't as Denovan told it!'

Kerry's face reddened slightly. 'That's nothing to

do with it,' she remarked, crossing her fingers behind her back at the white lie.

'Well, then?'

Kerry thought of the long succession of weekends that stretched out before her, blank and horribly empty. Perhaps after all it might be a good idea to go out for the evening with Frank—he was only trying to show how grateful he was. And just because he'd asked her out for a meal it hardly meant a lifelong commitment!

She sighed. 'Well, thanks, then, Frank. I'll look forward to that.'

Frank gave a little nod of satisfaction and went out.

Kerry pushed all thoughts of both O'Mara brothers out of her head, and settled down to the everyday life of a country GP.

The woman sitting opposite Kerry was slim, well dressed and very attractive—the kind of woman who carried herself with poise and confidence, who sat on committees and volunteered for charities. Only she wasn't poised at the moment. She twisted a handkerchief round in her hands perpetually, her face seemed pinched and her eyes were red, as if she'd been crying.

Kerry thought she could take an educated guess as to why Lady Bethany Hood was in such a state—it had only been a few days ago that her husband, Sir Vernon, had come in to confess that he was a drug user and to ask Kerry's help to kick the habit. He'd told her he'd already confessed all to his wife.

'What's the matter, Lady Hood?' she said gently. 'I very rarely see you in the surgery.'

'Please call me Bethany.' The woman put a hand up to a stray lock of hair over her forehead and brushed it back nervously. 'Oh, dear, I don't know really why I came. I doubt there's anything anyone can do anyway…'

'Why don't you try me?' suggested Kerry. She pushed a box of tissues over the desk towards the distraught woman, who now had tears pouring down her face.

'You…you're not going to believe this. I couldn't believe it at first…'

Her voice trailed off and she looked at the floor as if looking for the words to convey her distress. Kerry waited patiently. It was no good hurrying someone on in these circumstances.

Then Bethany took a deep breath and said shakily, 'It's my husband…you probably know he's the MP for this area? Recently he seems to have changed. He used to have quite a sunny disposition, but now he seems moody and taciturn. I'd thought it was pressure of work—he's home so seldom and seems to be on so many committees. Then he…he told me out of the blue that he's been taking drugs…he's addicted to them!' Bethany dabbed at her eyes with the tissue. 'I feel as horrified as though he'd threatened me with a gun, and completely bewildered…'

She stopped talking for a second and looked perceptively at Kerry. 'I guess he's already been to see you, hasn't he?' Then she sighed. 'Don't answer that—it's patient confidentiality, isn't it? I suppose I must be thankful that he realised he had to get professional help.'

'At least he has told you—that must have taken some courage.'

Bethany looked at Kerry sceptically. 'Courage, you

think? More like he's just frightened I'll find out from someone else…the papers perhaps! The fact is, Doctor…' her sad eyes met Kerry '…I've put up with a lot over the years one way or the other, but I never dreamed that he'd resort to drugs. I love him. Don't ask me why, but I do, despite everything, and I'm not going to let my marriage break up without a fight. I want to know if it's possible for this rehab to work and how I can help him.'

Vernon Hood didn't know how lucky he was to have such a strong wife, reflected Kerry. 'I think with your support he'll do well,' she said. 'He'll have bad days and good days, and you'll have to ride those out. Make sure he goes to the centre—they'll need to do regular blood tests to check that he's keeping his side of the bargain.'

Bethany nodded and said bitterly, 'I can't understand him—a man who has everything fooling around with things I'd be shocked that my teenage son would take, let alone a mature man.' Her voice hardened. 'He says he's going to rehab and he'll never take them again but I don't know that I believe him.'

Kerry leaned back in her chair, thoughtfully drumming her pencil on the desk. 'You know, Bethany, this might be a good time to get your husband more involved in local issues. What could be better at this time than when everyone's trying to get back to normal after the flood? It might take his mind off his problem. I'm thinking perhaps of a fundraising event for people who've been very badly affected.'

Bethany said slowly, 'Could be a good idea. You mean like a garden party or something? I suppose we could have it in our garden—invite the whole village to come, and have cake stalls, things like that!'

'Absolutely. People need something to bring them together after the trauma Braxton's suffered. And if you need an extra pair of hands, I'll be willing to help.'

Bethany gave a watery smile. 'You know, this is perhaps the focus that could help Vernon and I get together again. He's not been involved in many local issues recently…' Her voice trailed off, then she stood up resolutely and said, 'I feel so much better. Thank you so much for listening to me.'

'Any time you need me, I'm here. As I said, you will go through bad patches, but please don't struggle on thinking no one can give you any help.'

Bethany looked quite different as she left the room, walking with quite a spring in her step, obviously motivated to cope with her husband and start a new project. *Let's hope my advice works,* thought Kerry wryly.

The Pear and Partridge was the local pub and had been badly affected by the flood, but had now reopened again. Frank and Kerry had to fight their way through a jolly crowd of people round the bar to one of the tables at the end of the room.

'I'm sorry this isn't in quite the same league as the Farmer's Plough,' apologised Frank. 'The trouble is, I can't drive for a while, and the Farmer's Plough was booked up.'

'This is fine, Frank. Don't worry.'

They sat down and Frank smiled at her. 'I'd like to have taken you somewhere more special—I know it's your birthday today.' He reached in his pocket, brought out a slim, gift-wrapped parcel and passed it over the table to her. 'Just a little thought and a sort of thank-you for all your work,' he murmured.

Kerry gazed at it in surprise. 'You shouldn't have done this, Frank.'

He watched as she undid it and pulled out a beautiful silk scarf in soft rainbow colours. 'That's lovely, Frank…very kind.' Her voice trailed off, slightly embarrassed.

He leaned forward over the table. 'I thought it would suit your colouring. And I'm so glad you could come out tonight—it gives us a chance to get to know each other properly. I guess we've been leading different lives.'

'I suppose so,' replied Kerry, rather uneasily. She didn't know if it was necessary to know each other 'properly' in order to work together—things seemed to be moving on to a more personal footing than she wanted.

She looked at him brightly. 'Anyway, it's a good chance to discuss our thoughts on getting some help in the practice—Liz Ferris is keen for us to get another practice nurse.'

The waiter poured some wine into Frank's glass and he took a sip, nodding his approval of it. 'Oh, I don't think we want to talk shop tonight, do we?' he said easily. 'I'd rather talk about you and how you've been faring this year since poor Andrew's death. I feel I've rather left you to get on with your life since he died. It must have been so difficult for you.'

Why was Frank suddenly bringing this subject up? Kerry didn't want to talk to him about Andy—she knew she'd moved on from that tragedy.

'I've put that behind me, Frank,' she said firmly, taking a long drink of wine.

'Good, good. That's a great step forward. A new life ahead of you!' He smiled broadly at her, a smile that sat strangely with his austere features. 'Now, what would you like to eat?'

'A steak would be nice, with a salad.'

While Frank waved the waiter over, Kerry's mind drifted back to the evening she'd spent with Denovan only a few nights ago and the fizzing electric tension there'd been between them, the way they'd kissed so passionately and then the unbelievably wonderful ending when they'd done much more than kiss. Like the re-winding of a film, she recalled every passionate frame, stamped for ever in her mind—so very different from this mundane evening with Frank.

Frank's voice intruded on her thoughts. 'So, have you heard from Denovan recently?' he asked casually.

'Oh, yes. He's told me he's contemplating taking this new job—quite a good offer, I think.'

Frank nodded, a wry smile on his face. 'Denovan was always born to do well,' he said quietly.

Kerry looked at him in surprise—there was almost a hint of pride in Frank's voice. Perhaps underneath the veiled criticisms and anger with each other, there was a kind of love between them after all.

Kerry took a sip of wine and looked at Frank over the rim of her glass. She took a chance to speak bluntly. 'It can't have been easy, having a young brother and a stepmother suddenly break into your world, Frank. You must have felt very isolated.'

He nodded. 'Yes, that about sums it up. We both have hot tempers, I guess—but I'll be honest. I wish we were closer, and I'm glad and surprised Denovan came up when I was in hospital.' He looked slightly shamefacedly at Kerry. 'We were out of order, quarrelling in front of you the other day, but we find it difficult to communicate.'

'So I've noticed,' said Kerry with a grin.

He smiled back at her, the atmosphere lightening somewhat. 'Changing the subject, I wanted to know if you've ever been to the Opera House in Buxton?'

'Oh, yes, it's absolutely lovely.'

'They've got a very good programme this summer. I wonder if you'd like to come to one of their concerts— I think you'd enjoy it.'

Frank seemed to be making a pass at her, Kerry thought in astonishment. There had never ever been any inkling of that before his accident. She looked across at him appraisingly and saw a lonely, middle-aged and rather sad man, weakened through illness, with no other family except Denovan, and probably suddenly aware how time was passing. How could she get out of any future dates without offending him? She didn't mind being his friend, but she didn't want to encourage him in any other kind of relationship.

'I'm sure I'd love it,' she said vaguely, then tried to change the subject. 'I'm looking forward to seeing my mother tomorrow—I haven't seen her for ages. I thought I'd take her over to Dovedale and Hardwick Hall.'

To her relief their conversation turned to the other delights of Derbyshire and Kerry began to relax.

He'd made it! Driving through London on a Saturday evening had been a nightmare, but once he'd got onto the motorway it had been reasonably free of traffic. Denovan hummed to himself happily as he drew up on the road outside Kerry's cottage. The light was on in the living room, although the curtains were drawn. It was her birthday and he'd been determined to surprise her. He pictured her face as he appeared at the door. He'd learned by chance from Freda that it was Kerry's birthday, when she'd shown him a card she'd got for Kerry that she thought was particularly hilarious. When Kerry had said she couldn't come to London, he'd known he had to see her anyway. Archie had been very happy to stay with his childminder for the night.

Until now he'd come to the conclusion that he would never find anyone he'd love—hadn't really cared whether he did or not. Somehow relationships with women didn't seem to work with him and anyway, with Archie to think of, she had to be an ultra-special person who loved children, and would love Archie especially.

And then he'd met Kerry! During the last few days away from her it had hit him like a thunderbolt that he'd found that special person. He grinned happily. Kerry was perfect—fun, beautiful, kind, and their lovemaking had been wonderful. He wondered if she'd missed him as much as he'd missed her. He couldn't wait to see her—to tell her that he loved her and that he wasn't going to sign that contract after all.

He unclipped his safety belt and was about to open the car door when he noticed two figures strolling up to the front door of the cottage. In the light streaming through the fan light of the door he could see that one of them was Kerry, and the other, to his surprise, was Frank.

'What's she doing with him?' he asked himself.

Then he thought that it had to be something to do with work—probably they'd had a meeting at the surgery with the other staff. He would wait to get out of the car until Frank had gone—he didn't particularly want to see him so soon after their last acrimonious encounter.

He wound down his window to see them more clearly and their voices floated over to him.

Kerry was saying, 'It's been a lovely evening, the food was delicious—and thank you for the lovely present. You really didn't need to buy me anything.'

'It was my pleasure,' Frank replied. 'I've enjoyed every minute of it. I hope we can do it again very soon. Perhaps Buxton Opera House next time?'

Frank leant forward and brushed Kerry's cheek with his lips, and Denovan watched with disbelief and a feeling of angry bewilderment. They obviously hadn't had a meeting regarding work—it had been just the two of them, out for dinner!

Denovan ran a distracted hand through his hair. She knew the background of how things were between him and Frank—how could she, only days later, allow the man to kiss her, arrange future outings? Only two nights ago he and Kerry had been in each other's arms, making passionate love in that very cottage. Surely she was aware that he thought she was very special, that they were more than just good friends?

Denovan stared transfixed at the tableau of the two of them smiling at each other, at Frank patting her cheek before he turned away, and a crashing disappointment overtook him. Denovan had been under the illusion for the past few days that he and Kerry were special to each other, and that there was no one else in her life. It was almost like a betrayal, he reflected bitterly.

Now he knew just why she was so busy that she couldn't come to London this weekend—she was busy dating his brother while he was out of the way! It hadn't taken her long to fasten on to Frank, he thought savagely. Now he came to think of it, she'd often seemed sympathetic towards his brother. Perhaps Frank had always been in her sights, and now he was back from hospital, available, and the coast was clear.

Frank was walking away down the street now. Denovan watched him disappear and stared at the closed door of the cottage. Well, he wasn't going to be cast away like an old glove—off with the old, on with the new! He wanted an explanation—he'd come all the way from London and he wasn't going to creep back without knowing precisely what Kerry was up to!

He leapt out of the car and slammed the door shut, then strode angrily towards the cottage. The light was still on in the lounge and he rapped on the front door. A few seconds later Kerry opened it and a look of amazed delight spread over her face.

'Denovan! What on earth are you doing here?'

For a second he hesitated, stunned again by her beauty, the happy look of welcome on her face, then he pushed past her into the little room. He wasn't going to have a row with her on the doorstep. He whipped round to look at her, his face a grim mask.

'I know now why you were too busy to see me this weekend,' he grated. 'While the cat's away, the mice play! Why didn't you tell me you were involved with Frank, of all people? Why did you lead me on?'

CHAPTER TEN

THERE was deathly silence, except for the ticking of the clock in the kitchen and Denovan's words ringing in the air.

Kerry's welcoming expression changed to one of incredulity. She was speechless for a moment, then she gathered herself together.

'*Lead you on?*' she said, her horrified eyes wide with disbelief. She shook her head helplessly. 'I don't know what you're talking about,' she said at last.

The blue eyes flashed at her. 'Do me a favour, Kerry—in future tell me the truth!'

Kerry looked at Denovan's thunderous face. Suddenly he'd become the man she'd first encountered over the phone only three weeks ago—arrogant and surly, his charm and charisma put firmly on the back burner. She wasn't about to take that from anybody.

'Don't insult me, Denovan. I've never lied to you!'

'You told me you couldn't come to London because your mother was coming to see you—you never mentioned that the real reason was because you were seeing Frank. You might have told me that you and he were more than colleagues.'

'I didn't mention it because it isn't true! He kindly

asked me out to thank me for all the hard work I've put in while he's been in hospital. And please don't dare come and tell me who I can see and can't see. As far as I'm aware, I'm a free agent.'

His eyes locked with hers stonily. 'So our little liaison the other night meant very little to you, then? I was just a ship passing through the night, a bit of fun, was I?'

'This is utterly ridiculous,' she snapped, treacherous tears of fury and frustration welling up in her eyes. She loved this man, she wanted him like crazy, but not like this, accusing her of betraying him, of treating their lovemaking so lightly.

She drew herself up to her full height and looked at Denovan scornfully. 'I don't have to defend myself. I'd like to know why I can't go out with my practice partner if I want. It's absolutely no one else's business… he's purely a colleague.'

'It didn't look that way. I thought you never went out with him socially?'

'I don't—this is the first time I've had dinner with him. As I said, he was grateful to me. I don't have to apologise to you or anyone for spending an evening with Frank.'

'Don't be fooled by him, Kerry—he's a con man.'

Kerry almost stamped her foot on the floor. 'Oh, for heaven's sake, Denovan, change the record! I'm sick of you both denigrating each other.' She looked at him coldly and pointed to the open door. 'Please leave. If you think I'm untrustworthy, perhaps we'd better call a halt to our friendship.'

Denovan glowered at her. 'Don't worry, Kerry—I

know when I'm not wanted. I thought we had something good going between us. Obviously I was wrong.'

This was so unutterably stupid. 'I too thought we
had something very special...' Kerry's voice faltered.

'If you'd thought anything of me at all, you wouldn't
have gone out with the one man who helped to ruin my
life. Why choose Frank, of all people?'

He strode out, and Kerry went to the doorway, her
blood boiling with disbelief and anger.

'You can't let the past go, can you?' she shouted
as his retreating back. 'This isn't about me and you.
This is about you and Frank and what went wrong in
the past!'

She watched as he turned to look at her briefly
before he got into the car and accelerated away in a
spray of pebbles. The hot tears that streamed down her
cheeks weren't just tears of anger but of sadness that
everything seemed to have gone wrong between them.

It had started to pour with rain, but Denovan hardly
noticed as he whipped through the dark countryside.

'What have I done?' he groaned, his hands grip-
ping the steering wheel until the knuckles were white.
The image of Kerry's slender figure in the doorway
and the heart-rending expression on her face stamped
themselves on his mind. 'What a fool I've been...' Cold
reality hit him forcefully, sickeningly. 'Kerry's right.
I've allowed what happened between Frank and me to
ruin any future I might have had with her.'

A lorry blared its horn at him as he rounded a corner
in the middle of the road and the vehicle behind flashed
its lights. He was in no fit state to drive—he knew that.
He drove into a layby and parked the car, then put his
arms on the wheel and rested his forehead on them. No

doubt about it, Kerry and he were finished, and it was all his fault. How could he have said all those horrible things to her, accusing her of betraying him, telling lies? He loved her, dammit, probably had done almost since the first day they'd met. And now it was all over, his ungovernable, unreasonable behaviour putting an end to any dream he had of marrying the most wonderful woman he'd ever met. No woman would put up with the way he'd treated Kerry.

And why did he hate his brother so? It had been years ago that his mother had left, and after all Frank had still been a teenager. Sadly he reflected that both he and his brother had suffered tragedies, both without mothers and a father who hadn't had the time or the patience to look after them or give them the love and security they needed. He, Denovan, had to learn to forgive and forget. He was poisoning his own life, and had allowed jealousy to destroy any love Kerry might have felt for him.

He gazed bleakly ahead of him through the lashing rain on the windscreen. Sadly he thought that if he wasn't careful he'd be so wrapped up in his own troubles that it would affect his son. He had to pull himself together and restart his life in London, accept the contract and be damn glad he had such a good job. Until three weeks ago he'd not had a thought of leaving London, and now he'd got to get back to that mind set and pick up where he left off.

Wearily he started the car again and started the long drive back to London.

Somehow Kerry got through the next week, plastering a smile on her face to mask her sadness. She presumed that Denovan had gone straight back to London, because he was certainly nowhere to be seen in Braxton the next day. She felt numb and bewildered that he should imagine she had betrayed him by going out with Frank—and it was so unfair, because she hadn't wanted to go out with Frank anyway!

She decided halfway through the week that she would write to Denovan—emails were too glib somehow. She would explain that she'd had no idea that Frank would look on their evening together as a prelude to other outings: and she would tell Denovan that she could understand why he was upset that she had gone out with his brother, but the evening had meant nothing to her. And finally she resolved that, foolish or not, she would tell Denovan that she loved him—put her cards on the table. Yes, he could be totally unreasonable and he could be arrogant and overbearing, but he could be so tender, so loving and such fun—she wasn't going to let him go out of her life without a fight!

She switched on the television to watch the news as she settled down with paper and pen to compose something she hoped would build bridges between Denovan and herself.

Drumming her pen on the table as she pondered what to write, Kerry vaguely caught the news headlines—a fire in the Midlands, strikes in Europe, a woman who'd received a bravery award… Then a presenter introduced someone who was taking up some important new job. A tall, dark, impossibly good-looking man with startling blue eyes stood by her side. Kerry drew in a breath of shock, dropping her pen in astonishment as a shot of Denovan, debonair and smiling, appeared on the screen!

An excited presenter thrust a microphone under his nose. 'I believe you're the new star who's going to front the new daily magazine programme on health matters?' she stated enthusiastically.

'That's right—we'll be covering concerns that people have over every aspect of health, with advice and information from agencies all over the world. We want to present it from all sorts of places—hospitals, villages in Africa, surgeries in South America—and we're going to make people aware not only of the latest technology but also the old-fashioned remedies that have proved successful.'

'It sounds as if it will be very interesting.'

'I'm sure it will. I'm looking forward to doing it immensely. I'll be travelling all over the world.'

The presenter asked him other questions, but Kerry hardly heard them. She was transfixed, staring at Denovan's image. He looked thinner, slightly drawn, perhaps a bit tired, but he was still the drop-dead gorgeous man who'd made love to her only a few days ago. The man she couldn't get out of her head—or her heart.

Then he gave that familiar heart-stopping smile into the camera, and his figure faded from the screen and a sports item took over. For a few seconds Kerry stared numbly at the screen without seeing anything on it, then slowly she got up and switched off the television.

So Denovan had finally decided to stay in London, to take on this wonderful contract—not that she blamed him for that, but somehow it was so very final. He had said before that he would let her know of his plans—it looked like he wasn't going to bother, and where would he find time for her in his new life? He'd looked cheerful and positive, clearly not suffering as she was.

Kerry snatched up the half-written letter and tore it into shreds. He was starting his life again without her—so she would do the same without him!

The Hoods' garden was a lovely one, with herbaceous borders curving round spacious green lawns that swept down to a small copse. It was late spring, and there was a haze of light green over the hedges and trees, the sun stronger now as it rose higher in the sky.

A bustling crowd filled the lawn, children shrieking with excitement as they bounced on a bouncy castle, and a little roundabout in a corner of the garden was attracting lots of small visitors. In ten days Vernon and Bethany Hood had mobilised an army of volunteers to help raise money for victims of the floods, and there were cake stalls, trestle tables groaning with secondhand books, and a section filled with donated plants to be sold.

There was an air of jollity about the place, a renewed sense of optimism after the tragedy of the flooding, and it seemed the only person who wasn't happy, reflected Kerry gloomily, was her! She fixed a smile on her face as she helped to serve coffee and tea, but inside she felt as churned up as colours in a kaleidoscope—for the whole week she'd been unable to stop thinking of the terrible night when Denovan had appeared and accused her of betraying him. It was so unjust! She hadn't wanted to go out with Frank particularly, but why should she stay in like a nun, just because Denovan wasn't around?

Her future with Denovan had seemed so vague. He'd given her no promises. Surely if he'd really loved her, he'd have told her so? When he'd returned to London with Archie, she'd known that he was contemplating taking this new job, and that perhaps their little love affair wouldn't last as far as he was concerned. But there'd always been hope that he wouldn't drop her completely, and might eventually realise how much she meant to him. Now that hope seemed to have been dashed completely.

Now she'd made up her mind—she was going to get a job somewhere else. Working with Frank and the perpetual reminder of Denovan, by association, was too much for her. She owed the people of Braxton a lot, but they would get someone else who would come to love the area as much as she did, and work with more enthusiasm than she could bring to the village now. She needed a fresh start, something to engage her mind that would obliterate any thoughts of Denovan. She had already contacted an agency that was recruiting doctors for jobs in Australia. She hadn't told Frank yet—she would give him time to get back on his feet—but she had mentioned it to Daphne one morning before anyone else had come in. Daphne had gazed at Kerry in disbelief then she'd given a sudden hoot of realisation.

'Aha! It's Denovan, isn't it? You and he are getting together? I knew all along he was mad about you—he never stopped looking at you when you were in the room. I thought there was something going on! I suppose you're going to join him in London, then?'

Kerry had managed to mumble, 'No, I'm not going to London. The job is in Australia.'

'What? Australia?' Daphne had gasped. 'Wow! What a place to settle down together!'

'Not…not together, Daphne, I'm afraid. By myself.'

Daphne had frowned. 'But why go so far away?

I thought you loved it here. Oh, you will be missed. You're the best doctor we've ever had! No one else listens like you do. Why on earth are you going there?' Her round, kindly face had been filled with concern, then she'd looked perceptively at Kerry's pale face and said slowly, 'What's going on, lovey? There's more to this than wanting a new job, isn't there?'

Kerry had shaken her head wordlessly, but her anguished face had given her away.

'Oh, Lord, it is Denovan O'Mara, isn't it? What's happened? I was positive you and he were falling in love.'

Kerry had swallowed a lump in her throat and said in a small voice, 'I thought we'd got something going too, Daphne, but whatever it was, it's over now, and although I love him, he definitely doesn't need me, so… I don't know, I feel I need to start again.'

'Oh, you poor love.' Daphne put her arm round Kerry and hugged her. 'He must be mad not to see that you were meant for each other. But please, Kerry, please don't do anything in a hurry. It's only been a few days since Denovan left. Give it time before you make such a drastic decision.'

But the decision had been made—she'd set the ball rolling before she could change her mind, and now she gazed abstractedly across the garden, vaguely watching everyone milling around the stalls, their happy chatter a background to her sad thoughts.

'Any chance of a coffee, Dr Latimer?'

Kerry jumped out of her reverie to see Vernon Hood standing in front of her. He looked slightly embarrassed, bunching his hands in his pockets, a wary look on his face as if he was uncertain what sort of reception he was going to get from her.

'Certainly you can have some coffee,' said Kerry, smiling at him. 'You and your wife have done a marvellous job here—it's just what the village needed to cheer them up!'

He took the cup of coffee from her and put in a spoonful of sugar, stirring it in thoughtfully.

'I took your advice,' he said in a low voice. 'I'm finding it difficult, but I have stuck to the plan.' He glanced across to his wife, who was selling sweets at the sweet stall. 'Bethany's been marvellous. She told me she'd been to see you. I just wanted to thank you for suggesting this, it's given us something to do together.'

A child came running up, shouting to Vernon, 'Come on, Daddy, come on! Come and guess how many sweets are in the jar. If you get it right, we win it!'

Kerry smiled at Vernon. 'Looks like you have plenty to keep you occupied. And I must say you've done a fantastic job getting all this organised.'

She watched the little girl drag her father off to the sweet stall, and Vernon putting his arm round his wife when he got there. Perhaps he would manage to get drug-free after all and get his life back together again. She smiled to herself, the first feelings of optimism starting to stir inside her. If Vernon Hood could get his life back together, so could she! Roll on, Australia!

The stalls were being dismantled now, the bunting unhooked from the trees, and the crowds were beginning to disperse. Kerry lugged a large sack with used polystyrene cups and plates back to the bins by the house where the volunteers were clearing away.

'Kerry! Kerry! Hello!'

The voice was a child's and had a rather familiar ring to it. Kerry put the sack down and turned round. She could hardly believe her eyes as she watched Archie O'Mara scampering across the lawn towards her, his little face wreathed in a happy grin, a large football in his arms.

'Look what I've won,' he panted, looking at her gleefully through his round metal-rimmed glasses. 'I scored a goal in the net—you get a football if you do that.'

'Archie! How lovely to see you. I thought you were in London.'

'We had to come back for something important, so I'm staying with Larry and Daphne.'

'Did...did they bring you here today?'

'No, Daddy did!'

Kerry looked around the garden, her heart pounding like a drum against her ribs. Was Denovan here—was she about to bump into him?

'Where is he now?' Her voice sounded rather breathless.

'Somewhere over there,' shouted Archie carelessly, throwing the ball in the air and kicking it hard down the lawn.

Kerry looked in the direction he'd indicated, and there, standing under the trees and looking at her, was Denovan. As she watched, he started to walk towards her with a sense of purpose, his eyes never leaving her face, steady, unblinking, an unreadable expression in their clear blue depths.

Why was he coming towards her? What could he possibly have to say to her that hadn't been said before? Kerry's mouth went dry and she felt a prickling sensation at the back of her neck.

He stood in front of her, and Kerry looked up at him wordlessly, her eyes drinking in every aspect of him—his athletic figure, his strong, mobile face and firm lips. He was just as she'd been dreaming about him every night since he'd left.

'Why are you going to Australia?' he asked very quietly. 'I didn't know that was in the pipeline.'

She stared at him and said stupidly, ignoring his question, 'Why are you back here? I thought you were about to start this amazing new job?'

'Possibly.'

Kerry frowned. 'I don't understand. And how do you know that I'm going to Australia? I haven't told anyone except for... Daphne! Did she tell you?'

A glimmer of smile touched his lips. 'She mentioned it,' he admitted. 'When do you go?'

'I don't know yet.'

'So it's not been finalised yet?'

'There's a lot of paperwork to do.' She bit her lip. 'You didn't answer my question. I asked why you'd come back—Archie said it's for something important?'

'It is important, but I'd rather not discuss it here. Do you mind if we take a walk around the field at the back of the garden?'

'Surely, Denovan, we've nothing left to say to each other?'

He took her arm. 'Oh, yes, we do,' he said firmly, guiding her to the gate that led to the field.

They were alone, just the wind whispering through the trees and a lark somewhere high above them singing his soaring song. Kerry's heart hammered against her ribs, a million unanswered questions jumbling in her mind.

'What's this all about, Denovan, this very important thing you want to tell me? We're not friends now—remember?'

He put his hands on her shoulders and looked intently into her eyes. 'You have every reason not to be my friend any more,' he said huskily. 'I've been such a damn fool. You see, I realised I'd blown our relationship sky high—messed up with you completely. I thought it was the end between us. Then I got a phone call…'

'A phone call?' echoed Kerry. She frowned up at him. 'What about?'

'It was from Daphne, and she put it bluntly—she wanted to know what on earth I'd been saying to you. And then she told me something rather amazing.'

'Amazing?' Kerry began to sound like an echo chamber, repeating everything that Denovan said.

'She said that after all that had happened she got the impression you might still be rather…fond of me?' Denovan's eyes never left Kerry's face. 'I want to know—is she right?'

Kerry started to tremble, a sudden little chink of happiness pushing its way into her sadness. 'What gave her that impression?' Her voice was shaky.

'She said you were very sad that we'd parted, and that you'd told her you'd thought we had something special together.' He smiled wryly. 'She said I was a fool—and she was right. Then she told me you were going to Australia—and it hit me like a bombshell. I suddenly realised I couldn't bear it—couldn't bear having you so far away from me.'

'Daphne seems to have told you a lot of things,' said Kerry with some asperity, but inside her the little chink of happiness had become a huge beam, flooding through her, bubbles of euphoria threatening to burst out in a big shout of delight! She opened her mouth to speak again, but he put a finger on her lips.

'Let me have my say, please, Kerry. I know I've hurt you, thrown many insults at you. I don't deserve it, but I want to know—can you ever forgive me for being so boorish, saying you'd betrayed me, told me lies?' Then he added softly, putting his finger under her chin and lifting her face towards his, 'Please, my darling Kerry, give me another chance. I love you so very much—and I want you to be the centre of my world and Archie's. I want us to be together for ever.'

His hands on her shoulders tightened, and he pulled her towards him, looking down into her eyes. 'And if you won't give me another chance,' he added firmly, 'I won't take no for an answer anyway. Archie and I will follow you anywhere you go until you say yes!'

And the big bubble of joy burst inside Kerry and she threw back her head and laughed. 'Then I'll have to forgive you, won't I?' she gulped, brushing away the happy tears that poured down her cheeks.

She wound her arms round Denovan's neck and smiled at him. 'And tell me, where is our world going to be?' she asked. 'London?'

He shook his head. 'I think it's about time I made it up with my brother, don't you? I'm coming back to Braxton Falls, back to my roots, and I'll apply for the job of new partner—if Frank will have me!'

'I think Frank would like you to be friends,' said

Kerry. 'Despite everything, I think there's a bond there you haven't realised.'

Denovan grinned. 'I'll tell him that I'm very grateful to him—after all, if he hadn't crashed his car and gone to hospital, I might never have met you! I owe him everything.'

There was a loud bang and a football came hurtling over the hedge, followed by a small boy scrambling through the gate. Archie looked crossly at his father and Kerry.

'Where have you two been?' he demanded. 'I've been looking all over the place for you.'

Denovan crouched by his little son and put his arm round his waist. 'I've got a bit of news for you,' he said. 'We're going to move from London and live here with Kerry—what do you think of that?'

Archie looked solemnly at his father. 'For ever? Near Larry and Daphne?'

'Yes.'

The little boy turned a somersault and laughed. 'That's cool, that is!' Then he looked up at them impishly. 'I'm very hungry—can we have a pizza?'

So they all went hand in hand to get a pizza.

EPILOGUE

THE sand was warm between Kerry's toes, and it stretched white and gleaming in a curve round the bay, where the waving palms rustled and the light wind made her filmy white kaftan billow out like a cloud about her. Beyond her the sea sparkled with myriad diamond drops in the hot sun, and under an awning in front of her she could see Denovan turning to watch her as she walked towards him on their wedding day.

By Denovan's side was Frank—how glad she was that he had consented to be best man. After all that had gone on between the two brothers, this was sweet indeed. And by her side, holding her hand and jumping up and down excitedly, was Archie, wearing stripy cotton shorts and a little straw hat. Sitting on chairs under the trees were her mother and sister, her mother dabbing tears of happiness from her eyes.

This was the island she'd thought she'd never get to, the dream she'd thought she'd lost when Frank had been injured. It was hard to believe that now, only a few weeks later, her life had turned round and she was miraculously marrying Denovan O'Mara in a place where 'golden sands fringed by waving palms and an azure sea' surrounded her.

Denovan took Kerry's hand as she came beside him and held it tightly. He didn't speak aloud, but she knew when his deep blue eyes held hers so tenderly that he loved her. And that was all she needed to know.

* * * * *

Mills & Boon® Hardback

June 2012

ROMANCE

A Secret Disgrace	Penny Jordan
The Dark Side of Desire	Julia James
The Forbidden Ferrara	Sarah Morgan
The Truth Behind his Touch	Cathy Williams
Enemies at the Altar	Melanie Milburne
A World She Doesn't Belong To	Natasha Tate
In Defiance of Duty	Caitlin Crews
In the Italian's Sights	Helen Brooks
Dare She Kiss & Tell?	Aimee Carson
Waking Up In The Wrong Bed	Natalie Anderson
Plain Jane in the Spotlight	Lucy Gordon
Battle for the Soldier's Heart	Cara Colter
It Started with a Crush...	Melissa McClone
The Navy Seal's Bride	Soraya Lane
My Greek Island Fling	Nina Harrington
A Girl Less Ordinary	Leah Ashton
Sydney Harbour Hospital: Bella's Wishlist	Emily Forbes
Celebrity in Braxton Falls	Judy Campbell

HISTORICAL

The Duchess Hunt	Elizabeth Beacon
Marriage of Mercy	Carla Kelly
Chained to the Barbarian	Carol Townend
My Fair Concubine	Jeannie Lin

MEDICAL

Doctor's Mile-High Fling	Tina Beckett
Hers For One Night Only?	Carol Marinelli
Unlocking the Surgeon's Heart	Jessica Matthews
Marriage Miracle in Swallowbrook	Abigail Gordon

Mills & Boon® Large Print
June 2012

ROMANCE

An Offer She Can't Refuse	Emma Darcy
An Indecent Proposition	Carol Marinelli
A Night of Living Dangerously	Jennie Lucas
A Devilishly Dark Deal	Maggie Cox
The Cop, the Puppy and Me	Cara Colter
Back in the Soldier's Arms	Soraya Lane
Miss Prim and the Billionaire	Lucy Gordon
Dancing with Danger	Fiona Harper

HISTORICAL

The Disappearing Duchess	Anne Herries
Improper Miss Darling	Gail Whitiker
Beauty and the Scarred Hero	Emily May
Butterfly Swords	Jeannie Lin

MEDICAL

New Doc in Town	Meredith Webber
Orphan Under the Christmas Tree	Meredith Webber
The Night Before Christmas	Alison Roberts
Once a Good Girl...	Wendy S. Marcus
Surgeon in a Wedding Dress	Sue MacKay
The Boy Who Made Them Love Again	Scarlet Wilson

Mills & Boon® Hardback
July 2012

ROMANCE

The Secrets She Carried	Lynne Graham
To Love, Honour and Betray	Jennie Lucas
Heart of a Desert Warrior	Lucy Monroe
Unnoticed and Untouched	Lynn Raye Harris
A Royal World Apart	Maisey Yates
Distracted by her Virtue	Maggie Cox
The Count's Prize	Christina Hollis
The Tarnished Jewel of Jazaar	Susanna Carr
Keeping Her Up All Night	Anna Cleary
The Rules of Engagement	Ally Blake
Argentinian in the Outback	Margaret Way
The Sheriff's Doorstep Baby	Teresa Carpenter
The Sheikh's Jewel	Melissa James
The Rebel Rancher	Donna Alward
Always the Best Man	Fiona Harper
How the Playboy Got Serious	Shirley Jump
Sydney Harbour Hospital: Marco's Temptation	Fiona McArthur
Dr Tall, Dark...and Dangerous?	Lynne Marshall

MEDICAL

The Legendary Playboy Surgeon	Alison Roberts
Falling for Her Impossible Boss	Alison Roberts
Letting Go With Dr Rodriguez	Fiona Lowe
Waking Up With His Runaway Bride	Louisa George

Mills & Boon® Large Print
July 2012

ROMANCE

Roccanti's Marriage Revenge	Lynne Graham
The Devil and Miss Jones	Kate Walker
Sheikh Without a Heart	Sandra Marton
Savas's Wildcat	Anne McAllister
A Bride for the Island Prince	Rebecca Winters
The Nanny and the Boss's Twins	Barbara McMahon
Once a Cowboy...	Patricia Thayer
When Chocolate Is Not Enough...	Nina Harrington

HISTORICAL

The Mysterious Lord Marlowe	Anne Herries
Marrying the Royal Marine	Carla Kelly
A Most Unladylike Adventure	Elizabeth Beacon
Seduced by Her Highland Warrior	Michelle Willingham

MEDICAL

The Boss She Can't Resist	Lucy Clark
Heart Surgeon, Hero...Husband?	Susan Carlisle
Dr Langley: Protector or Playboy?	Joanna Neil
Daredevil and Dr Kate	Leah Martyn
Spring Proposal in Swallowbrook	Abigail Gordon
Doctor's Guide to Dating in the Jungle	Tina Beckett

0612 GEN STD LP